PRANKENSTEIN vs YANKENSTEIN
by Andy Seed

fatfoxbooks.com

Illustra... ...n

D0273898

"Prankenstein vs Yankenstein is funny and fun in equal measure. Kids will thoroughly appreciate this naughty treat of a read. Drag them away at your peril."

Natasha Harding, The Sun's Book Columnist

"A fantastic sequel – the hilarious pranks will ignite the mischievous side of any child. A brilliant read."

Lee Harpin, Sunday Mirror

"It's funny and brilliantly written, with an exciting fast-pace plot. This book will grip even the most reluctant young reader."

Katie Nicholl, Mail on Sunday and Author

"Full of fun, this series is sure to appeal to anyone with a sense of humour! Prankenstein vs Yankenstein offers lots of action and laughs as it builds to a satisfying conclusion. An entertaining read."

Sue Wilsher, Federation of Children's Book Group

PRANKENSTEIN vs
YANKENSTEIN
by Andy Seed

Illustrated by Richard Morgan

To the children and staff of Longman's
Hill Primary School. AS.

To all the little pranksters everywhere. RM.

First published in 2015 by Fat Fox Books Ltd.

Fox's Den
Wickets, Frittenden Road
Staplehurst, Kent TN12 0DH
www.fatfoxbooks.com

ISBN: 978-0992872854

Fat Fox and associated logos are trademarks and/or
registered trademarks of Fat Fox Books Ltd.

Text copyright © Andy Seed 2015

Illustrations copyright © Richard Morgan 2015

The right of Andy Seed to be identified as the author
and Richard Morgan to be identified as the illustrator
of this work has been asserted.

A CIP catalogue record for this book is available
from the British Library.

Printed and bound by CPI Group (UK) Ltd.

Contents

1
A sweet prank

Soapy Thompson nudged his pencil and watched it roll off the edge of the heavy walnut dining table and onto the white carpet beneath. He glanced round and saw Ivette, the family's Spanish au pair cooking in the huge kitchen next door. His mum was in her study across the hall working and his dad was at his restaurant in town. Soapy dropped onto the floor and pretended to look for the pencil. With a swift movement he flipped open his school bag, reached inside and, stealing another glance around, plucked out a small paper-wrapped package and thrust it into his pocket.

He stood up and called through the doorway. "I've finished my homework, Mum."

"Have you done it carefully?" The voice was distant but powerful.

"Yes."

"Did you check it?"

"Yes."

"Are all of the spellings right this time?"

"Yes."

"Are you just saying yes to keep me quiet?"

"Ye… I mean, no! I have done it really well, honestly Mum. Can I go to my room now?"

"All right, but keep off that games console – I read an article that says children who play on them a lot grow up stupid and end up listening to that hop hip drivel."

It was no good quarrelling with his mum – she was a lawyer and always won arguments. She was also overprotective, annoying and didn't understand boys. But Soapy's friends said their mums were like that too so it must be normal, he reckoned. He ran upstairs and dumped his history book on the bed. He noticed that it said 'ugh Thompson' on the cover – some yob at school had kindly smudged out the first letter of his name, Pugh.

What a completely rubbish name for a boy, Pugh is. He wondered if he could go online and get it changed officially to his nickname, Soapy. No point in trying really – his mum would take him to court. He imagined the scene.

Judge: *Case number 478: Pug Thompson*
versus his Mother. Step forward, Pug.

Soapy: *The name is Pugh, m'lud.*

Judge: *Ah, I beg your pardon Spew.*

Soapy: *No, Pugh, like pew.*

Judge: *You like pew? Well that sounds just like*
your name anyway – I don't see why you
want to change it.

Mum: *Your Honour, his name is…*
P, U, G, H.

Judge: *What a delightful name. I had a dog*
called that. It fell down a manhole.

Mum: *Yes, he wishes to change this perfectly*
good name against his parents' wishes,
Your Honour.

Judge: *Frightful whelp. What to?*

Soapy: *Soapy.*

Judge: *Sophie? That's*
a gell's name,
dammit!

Soapy: *No, Soapy m'lud.*

Judge: *Ah, So Pi – it's*
some kind of
Chinese thing
is it? Well, it's

> *perfectly ridiculous. Case dismissed.*
> *And fine the scoundrel five guineas.*

Mum: *Thank you, Your Honour. I'll ensure*
> *further punishments too – he can miss*
> *the next Star Wars movie for a start.*

Soapy woke out of his daydream and remembered the secret package in his pocket. He crept to the bathroom across the landing and lifted a tube of toothpaste from the cabinet. Back in his room he pushed a chair against the door and piled some clothes and things on top to prevent sudden entry – if his mum tried to come in he would say he was tidying.

No, she wouldn't believe that. Rearranging the furniture was better: fung shooey or whatever it's called.

With great care he pulled the object from his pocket and placed it on his bed. Then he walked over to his bookshelves and reached for a DVD box: 'The History of Lace' – a present from his granny. Inside was a small folding penknife.

If Mum ever found out that Dad gave me this....

Sitting on his bed in front of the package, Soapy unfolded the lined A4 paper in which the

small round object was wrapped. There before
him was a chocolate cookie: an Oreo, no less.
He wasn't allowed biscuits at home and he picked
up the thing in wonder, grateful that his school
friends, the Estonian twins Arvo and Loogi, had
given it to him. It consisted of two dark, crumbly
discs with a white cream filling in between.
He longed to eat it but had other plans.

Soapy put down the biscuit and unfolded the
penknife. It was a 'Junior Cub Camper', barely
sharper than the cutlery downstairs but it was
none the less a knife. He held the Oreo in his left
palm and very tentatively pushed the blade down
into the soft white filling so that the two halves
fell open. He put one down and, gently holding
the other, scraped the sugary cream off its inner
surface onto the paper. He did the same with the
other piece and then with a wet finger dabbed
the filling into his mouth, letting it melt with
great pleasure.

The two halves of the dark biscuit were inviting
him to tuck in too, but he resisted. Instead, he
unscrewed the top from the toothpaste and squirted
a blob of the white paste onto one of the discs.
Adding a little more he then pushed down the

other half of the biscuit onto it, twisting it lightly so that the Oreo was restored to its former appearance. Soapy put it down and giggled at his handiwork. The prank was ready – the question now was simple. *Who would be the victim?*

2

Invasion

Soapy lay on his bed and imagined who he'd like to give the special Minty Colgate Oreo to the most. His mum? *Ha, she would never eat it anyway.* His dad would and might even enjoy the joke but he was always at his restaurant or playing golf. Arvo or Loogi would be perfect but they might just suspect something since they had given him the biscuit in the first place.

He was just considering Ivette (did they have Oreos in Spain?) when the sound of footsteps on the landing outside his door made him jump.

There was a rap at his door. "Soapy?"

It was Ivette. With astonishing speed he picked up the biscuit and hurled it under the duvet beneath him.

"Er, yeah?"

"Supper in five minutes," she called, then

walked away.

Soapy pulled back the duvet to reveal a sorry sight. The Oreo had been squashed into a pile of gooey crumbs. There was toothpaste sticking to the sheet beneath.

He sighed. *Why did I do that? It's wasted now – I'll never prank anyone with it.*

But as he cleaned up the mess he knew he was only kidding himself anyway. The sad truth was, that although Soapy Thompson loved pranks and knew loads of great ones, he'd never been daring enough to actually carry one out. Soapy knew it was his mum's fault mainly because she was just so, well, obsessed with health and safety and avoiding any kind of risk that life was totally boring. He understood that it was partly her law job that caused this but all the same – kids needed to have fun, he believed. *What harm could a few pranks do?*

As he mused on the unfairness of things, his mobile bleeped with a text from Arvo. At least he was allowed a phone, even if his mum had made it clear that it was mainly to help keep him out of danger when away from home.

The message said:

`To what are you up?`

Soapy was never quite sure if the Twince (as he called them) wrote like that deliberately. They were from Estonia but their English was good when they wanted it to be. He started keying back knowing that the message would be mangled by the ultra cheapo 'smartphone' that his dad had bought him from a dodgy market stall somewhere. The problem was that the predictive text was stuck – it came up with suggestions for what he was typing and wouldn't change them. Soapy wanted to write:

`Just wasted the Oreo by accident`

But his phone actually put:

`Justin washed the organ`
`by accelerating`

Arvo replied right away.

`What? Even we can't work that out!`

It was no good. Soapy called the Twince instead. Arvo put his mobile on speaker so Loogi could join in. He told them about the aborted toothpaste biscuit prank.

Arvo laughed. "Hey, you have been making a great discovery: a snack that rots your teeth and then cleans them. It could sell the squillions!"

"Yes but it wasn't my idea – I found it on the internet."

Loogi changed the subject. "Did you see earlier the footy, Soapy? Estonia beat Wales 3-1 in the Euro qualifier. Our dad was going nuts."

"No, missed it – my mum made me do homework."

"Whaaaat! It is being the first day of the Easter holidays. That is unfair. That is messing with your people rights!" cried Arvo.

"Human rights," corrected Loogi. "Or is it human wrongs?"

"She said it's because my aunt and uncle are coming over for most of the holidays."

"Ah yes," said Arvo. "These are the Americans with the girl cousin."

"Yeah, why can't they have a boy? And she's called Topazz – what sort of a name is that?"

"How old is this Toepad?" said Loogi.

"Twelve. A few months

older than me, annoyingly."

"But is she and her parents knowing that she is coming to the house of a monster?"

"Eh?"

Arvo laughed. "Oh, come on Soapy, I know it's nearly a year, but you can't have forgotten Prankenstein already."

Soapy looked about. "Shhhhh, you two – you know that's totally secret! Your parents might hear you."

"Relax, they are having beefy argument downstairs – we are hearing," said Loogi.

"Anyway," said Soapy, "Prankenstein is dead. We killed him, remember – or rather my mum did when she made me take the pills to stop my sleepwalking."

Arvo's voice dropped to suggest a hint of doom. "But you are still in the danger if you eat any cheese. It is this big allergy of yours that is problem. What if these visitors do their greeting with slabs of cheesiness? A website of reliability informs me that the average USA guy is eating his own weight of head in cheese every three weeks. Or something."

Loogi exhaled. "That is fool nonsense rubbish, brother. It is every two weeks. Anyway, even if they bring extreme cheese Soapy is not going to touch it so he cannot transform into that evil prank-playing beastie that brought much troubles to us last time."

"Exactly right," said Soapy. "Prankenstein is never coming to life again. I won't let him, he's out of control. I'm not sleepwalking anymore and so I'm not eating cheese in the night. He's finished."

Soapy was called for supper once again and he ended the call, his mind whirring with thoughts of Prankenstein, his dark, manic other self who he'd never met. *If only I could play pranks without turning into a wild, dangerous hairy creature...*

3
Topazz

The restaurant was quiet except for one large raucous table where Soapy sat with his mum and dad. Opposite them were his Aunt Dove, Uncle Finn and cousin Topazz. They had flown over from California the day before and were excitedly talking about all the things they'd like to do now they were in England, as they called Britain.

"London is top of my list," said Dove. "I want to see all the sights: Buck Palace, Big Ben, The Crown Jewels, and those crazy red soldier guys with the humongous hats."

Soapy was shocked at how young and attractive she was. His other aunts were quite old and dowdy but Aunt Dove was tanned and smiley with the kind of hair that he'd only seen before on shampoo adverts. She was loud but he liked her straight away – there was a kind of fascinating hippie

side to her character and appearance, and her jewellery was extravagant. And amusing.

Uncle Finn was Soapy's dad's younger brother. He was a giant: six foot six inches tall with a mop of fair hair. He looked like a kind of overwatered Boris Johnson.

"I haven't been on the London Eye, either," he boomed in a voice so deep that the plates rattled. He wasn't quite as sun-browned as the other two but he still looked supernaturally healthy. He was also quite rich, it seemed, running his own digital company. Soapy was delighted with the very cool bodyboard that Finn had given him as a present.

"Hey, I know the surf here's not quite California but get your dad to take you down to Cornwall with this," he'd said. "It'll be a bunch of fun, as they say in the States."

Soapy's dad seemed anxious to make a good impression especially as the meal was in his own restaurant. He opened another bottle of expensive wine and held up a hand.

"It's just as well that you're keen on London because we're going tomorrow morning. I've booked train tickets for all of us. We can spend the whole day there and come back in the evening."

"Hey, neat work, that's perfect," beamed Dove, revealing a set of blinding white teeth.

Soapy was just glancing at his cousin to try and suss her out when his mum called across. "Pugh, why don't you take Topazz over to the blackboard menu and choose a starter. We're going to be doing grown-up talk here, anyway." He knew he didn't have a choice.

Topazz gave him a little understanding smile and stood up. She was tall and tanned like her mother but with long blonde hair. She looked at least a year older than twelve and – Soapy couldn't deny it, *she looks kind of cool.*

"Hey," she said. "If we're not wanted then they're not wanted."

"Yeah," he grinned, feeling dim and suddenly shy.

"So, Dad told me you like to be called Soapy. What's that about?"

"Oh, when I was little I tried to wash my own hair at my granny's. I got the shampoo bit but couldn't manage the rinsing so she called me Soapy Head."

"Sweet little story. I like that you say 'granny' – we say grandma usually. I love the way you talk here."

"Do you like living in California, then?"

"It's cool – you must come over some day. San Francisco is great. We live by the beach so we do a lot of surfing and we have a jet ski. I play soccer too, and tennis and stuff. What are you into?"

Soapy tried to think quickly – all his interests sounded a bit dull in comparison. "I, er, like science and I'm really into playing pranks."

Her eyes lit up and she smiled, exposing another set of perfect polar-white teeth. "You're kidding me – I love science, and I'm so into pranks too! What kind of stunts do you pull?"

Soapy could see that she was really interested. "Well, just a couple of days ago I did this cool trick with an Oreo where you..."

She almost screeched with laughter. "Wait, don't tell me – not the toothpaste trick?"

He was amazed. "Yeah, do you know it?"

"I can't believe this. I saw it on the internet, right, and I did a full packet and left them on my dad's desk. He ate a whole one and spat it out all over the floor!

What happened with yours?"

Soapy gulped. "Well I made one just to test and I'm waiting to see who to prank, you know."

Topazz leaned her head to one side. "Ah, that's so sweet."

I wish I could tell her about Prankenstein. Then she wouldn't think I was so dull.

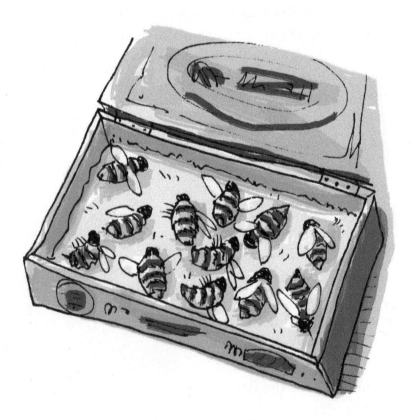

All he could think to say was, "I also like mountain biking, but Mum won't let me go anywhere that isn't flat."

She drew close and whispered, "Aren't parents just a sad sack of pants sometimes?"

Soapy laughed then blurted out. "And I collect bees."

Why did I say that?

Her big eyes lit up. "What, like honey bees? Do you have a hive-thing and stuff?"

"Well, no, just dead bees. They're really interesting under a microscope. I have twelve in a box in my room. You can just find them on the grass – they die of exhaustion..."

She touched his nose. "Soapy, you are so cute."

He looked down and gave an embarrassed smile just as his dad called over. "You kids chosen a starter yet? It's time to order – come on."

They walked back and Soapy thought that the Easter holidays were going to be a lot more interesting than usual.

4
Eggs are off

Soapy enjoyed the meal and he particularly liked the way that the conversation kept turning to the interesting differences between English words in the UK and USA. He also discovered something else about his glamorous American cousin when the time came to ordering the main course.

"I'd like the wild boar burger if it doesn't have any egg in it," said Topazz. "I'm really allergic to egg."

"Yeah, we have to be so careful – you'd be amazed how many foods contain egg," said Aunt Dove.

Soapy's dad jumped up. "Don't worry, I'll get the kitchen to do you one without egg."

As he disappeared, Soapy's mum bit her lip. "Oh dear, we'll be really, really careful. It must be a family thing – Pugh can't go near cheese. It's so difficult in restaurants, isn't it?"

Uncle Finn held up a palm and gave a wink.

"Hey, don't worry, we won't sue... Topazz has an EpiPen for emergencies anyway so she's safe."

Soapy leaned towards Topazz. "Have you ever had egg by accident?"

She lowered her voice to a whisper. "No, but I'm sometimes tempted, just to see what would happen. Shall I get you some cheese to liven up the evening?"

"NO!" Everyone suddenly looked round and Soapy blushed. "Er, no thanks, I'll just have the curry." Topazz sniggered into her napkin.

After they had all eaten, Soapy's dad went off to the toilet which prompted another round of conversation.

Topazz began. "Mom, can we start calling it 'the loo' from now on. I love that."

Aunt Dove chuckled. "No one back home will know what we're talking about."

"Don't you say 'bathroom'?" said Soapy.

"Yeah, 'washroom' or 'bathroom'," said Topazz. "Do you say 'lavatory'? That really cracks me up. It's too much like laboratory."

"It's better than calling it 'the john'," said Soapy, and Uncle Finn hooted.

"The whole 'pudding' thing here is weird, though," said Aunt Dove. "We just don't get that custard stuff you love."

Topazz stuck out her tongue. "I'm with you there, Mom – it looks tyrannosaurus gross!"

Soapy scrunched his face in mock protest. "You can't say that about custard – it's an insult to our nation."

"You're right there, kiddo," said his uncle. "These Americans can't complain about that when they have the silliest word for anything."

"That must be 'math'," said Soapy's mum with a slight wince.

"No, see my dazzling daughter's lovely hair?" said Finn. "She has a fringe – perfectly good word. But in the States they insist on calling it 'bangs'. I've been over there fifteen years and I still can't get used to that one."

"Hey, we gotta stand up against this," said

Dove to Topazz, who stuck out her lip. Soapy was laughing too much to notice. "Bangs! Really? *Bangs?*"

Back at home that evening, Soapy was lying on his bed still thinking how strange it was that he and his American cousin really liked each other when his mobile beeped with a text from the Twince.

> How was it going with the Americans?

Soapy texted `They are really nice` but his stupidphone spelt it as `Thermonuclear ark rear nicked` so he decided to video-call them on his laptop instead. Whilst it was connecting he tried keying the word 'Topazz' in his phone. It came out as 'Topsoil'.

Right, that's her nickname sorted.

Arvo was on screen as usual, with Loogi in the background doing a crossword or some other puzzle as he always was.

"So, they are wearing the Wild West frilly trousers and big Texas hats?"

"No, sadly," said Soapy. "But they are really fun, all three of them."

"Did Ivette like them as well?"

"Oh, she wasn't there – it's her birthday today so she went into town with friends."

Loogi looked up. "Your aunt is not being like your mother, then?"

Soapy chuckled. "Ha, about as different as you can get. She's kind of relaxed but with enormous hair. Her earrings are bigger than her head and she has this writing on her neck."

"Are you meaning tattoo?"

"Yes, unless it's graffiti by a very small and daring person."

"What is this writing saying?" asked Arvo.

"I couldn't read it but Topazz says it's the Sioux word for 'peace'."

Arvo's voice went up a notch. "Who is this Sue? Do you have another cousin?"

"Fool brother. Sioux is Indian tribe," said Loogi.

"Native Americans," added Soapy. "You know, those ones with the feathers and tipis who fight the cowboys in old films."

Arvo's voice rose even higher. "Your aunt is native warrior? Wow, can I have a go with her bow and arrow?"

"He is making the bogus remark now, Soapy," said Loogi hearing his friend laugh.

"She also has an eagle tattoo on her wrist but it looks more like a moody penguin."

"But is her name really Dove?" asked Arvo.

"Yes, it's a silly name but it could have been worse – Crow, maybe."

"How about Auntie Grouse?" giggled Arvo.

Soapy put on an American accent. "Hello, pleased to meet you. My name is Aunt Vulture."

Loogi brought his knowledge to the fore.

"There is also a bird called loon. And booby."

Soapy started to snigger uncontrollably imagining himself saying, 'Good morning Aunt Booby'.

Arvo continued. "Aunt Treecreeper is good. Hang on; Loogi is accessing the Google for more birds."

The exchange continued with the boys finding increasingly comical names until Soapy announced a winner. He was laughing so much that he didn't notice his bedroom door open.

"Right, that's it!" he roared.

"From now on she's Aunt Yellow-bellied Sapsucker!"

A throat-clearing noise made him turn round. His mother was peering in.

"Pugh, if you've quite finished, your uncle here is having a look round upstairs."

He shut off the call as his heart lost a beat. His mother's face was as cold as glass but his giant uncle slipped him a silent wink.

"Erm, I just need to, er, wash my hands," said Soapy scurrying away.

When the coast was clear, he checked his phone. A text from Arvo said:

What about your cousin Topazz?

He wanted to call them back and say she's friendly and funny and likes loads of great stuff and she's even into pranks and I think she likes hanging out with me, but he didn't dare for fear that they would laugh.

Instead he just started to type:

`She's cool.`

Then he realised that it would come out with 'shed coolant' or something equally senseless so he used hyphens.

`s-h-e i-s c-o-o-l.`

It worked. He went to bed imagining visiting California and zooming through the warm waters of San Francisco Bay on a jet ski with his cousin. As he drifted off to sleep Soapy didn't hear Ivette come in to the house carrying a white cardboard box containing cake, which she placed carefully in the fridge.

5
Toilet humour

Soapy was awoken by a loud rap on his door and the familiar strident voice of his mother.

"Seven o'clock! Remember we have to be on the train to London at half eight."

Oh yes, London, Americans, Topazz....

He turned over for one last brief snooze but felt something hard tugging at his left arm. Soapy reached across and touched what felt like a thick metal bracelet on his wrist.

Whaaat?

He threw back the duvet and screwed up his eyes to help them adjust to the light. What he saw made him think he must still be dreaming. Around his wrist was a heavy steel handcuff attached to a strong chain which trailed down the side of the bed. He leaned over to see where it went. The other handcuff was locked around something smooth and white that he couldn't make out. He pulled at the chain with both hands and saw the astonishing truth.

He was handcuffed to a toilet seat.

Soapy's first reaction was to think that the handcuffs must be toy ones or some kind of joke copy but even yanking hard at the clasps locking them together made no difference. They were solid metal real handcuffs. The one around the toilet seat wouldn't come off either – they were both properly locked.

Who could have done this? My cousin? Well, Topazz did say she liked pranks. But how could she have sneaked into my room without me noticing? Maybe it was Arvo and Loogi, finally getting revenge for all those shocking tricks that Prankenstein had played on them last year. *Wait. Hang on a minute. PRANKENSTEIN.*

*It couldn't be, could it? Did I accidentally eat
cheese at the restaurant? Prankenstein would
certainly have been able to pull off a mad stunt
like this and it's his kind of humour...*

But then Soapy came to his senses.

*How could it be Prankenstein? I'm Prankenstein!
He never pranks himself. And I remember taking
an anti-sleepwalking pill last night anyway. And
I don't have a headache like the last time it happened.*

It was a total mystery.

He sat up and wondered what to do. Could
he sneak into the garage and get Dad's tools out
to tackle the chain? At that moment Mum's voice
boomed up the stairs again.

"Get up right now, Pugh, or there'll be trouble!"

Trouble? There was going to be more than
trouble – how would he explain this to his parents?
And how do you get dressed with
a bog seat hanging from your arm?
He would have to try. He put the
seat on his bed, hoping it was clean,
and swung his legs round towards
where he left his slippers. At
least his feet were free. He found
the slippers and wiggled his

feet into them and right into something thick
and gooey and cold.

Ugh!

Instinctively Soapy jerked back his feet and
as he did so he saw flecks of a gloopy yellow
substance flick across his room, spattering the
carpet and furniture. He looked down at his toes
and saw that they were coated with something
very familiar. Custard.

What is going on?

He put a dab on his finger and sniffed it.
Unmistakably custard.

Who is doing this? What else is lying in wait?

He scanned the room inch by inch spying out
potential further pranks, using all of his knowledge
and experience. It did look like everything was
clear. He had to get to the bathroom and wash his
feet then clean up the mess. If Mum saw it she'd
do her nut.

With great difficulty, Soapy pulled on his
dressing gown and hid the heavy loo seat inside
it against his tummy. He glanced in the mirror
– it looked like he had swallowed the world's
largest pizza in one gulp. He would just have
to risk it. He edged open his door a fraction and

checked that the landing was clear. He scurried out with one hand hidden inside his robe like some kind of wounded war veteran trying to escape from hospital.

Leaving a trail of custard footprints he dived into the bathroom and rammed the door shut. As he did so, a cascade of small objects fell from the top of the door, landing with a series of sharp cracks that made Soapy yelp. When the noise stopped he looked down and saw eight little twisted blue packets each blasted open by a tiny explosion. Fun Snaps! His local joke shop called them 'Devil Bangers' – you threw them onto a hard surface and they popped satisfyingly. He'd been pranked a third time!

Now he knew how Prankenstein's victims felt. *But who is it?*

Fearing further tricks, he switched on the shower and tentatively stuck each foot under the spray of cold water. A voice made him jolt again.

"Mrs Thompson!"

It was Ivette. She was close, just on the landing outside the door.

"Where's the toilet seat gone?"

It was no use, he would just have to tell everyone what happened. With an overpowering sense of doom he pulled back the bolt on the door and let the toilet seat dangle from his arm. It really hurt.

He stepped out onto the landing and there was Ivette looking in the airing cupboard. When she saw Soapy, her eyes widened and her mouth formed a little 'O'. Then out of it came a roaring, gushing, screeching laugh followed by a loud Spanish exclamation. Everyone in the house came running.

6
Touring London with a toilet seat

Breakfast was mayhem.

After a ten minute bout of his parents raging and ranting (and suggesting that Soapy must have done the prank himself), there followed an intense session of googling where all four adults made suggestions for unlocking the handcuffs.

"It says here a bent paperclip will do it."

"This website reckons a hairgrip. What is a hairgrip?"

"Hey, there's a video here: 'Six Ways to Escape from Handcuffs'. Wait... have we tried smearing his wrists in butter? Hang on – is he wearing false padded wrists?"

"Hey, apparently you can get edible handcuffs."

"This one says use a key."

"Duh."

After unsuccessfully trying the better suggestions,

Soapy's dad spent a further ten minutes in the garage attacking the chain with a motley collection of saws, hammers, chisels, pliers, cutters and branch loppers. Most of them broke. He became increasingly short-tempered and violent with the tools.

"Dad, this hurts and you're going to chop my finger off if you carry on," squealed Soapy, turning his head away as his father lifted an axe then thought better of it.

"Just keep still and stop fussing."

"Fussing? I feel like one of Henry VIII's wives on Executioner Hill!"

At this point the enormous figure of Uncle Finn loped in. He had a turn at manically bashing the chain with the blunt chisel until flecks of sweat sprayed off his forehead.

"What about a drill?" said Soapy's dad.

"What about letting me live?" said Soapy.

Uncle Finn shook his head, put down the hammer and then picked up the toilet seat.

"Wait a minute, what are we doing? That chain is toughened steel – we'll never cut through it. We're approaching this all wrong. We should just break the toilet seat then at least Soapy will only have the handcuffs on until we can get someone to remove them. It's only plastic, look – it'll just break if we smash it against something hard."

Soapy's dad nodded his agreement and suggested bashing it on the big solid metal vice fixed to his work bench.

"Right," said Uncle Finn, gripping the seat and looking like he meant business. "Stand back, kid."

Soapy yelled, "I can hardly stand back when I'm chained to it!"

"OK, well, just turn away then."

Soapy did but he couldn't resist peeking out of one eye as the hulking uncle raised the toilet seat as high as he could above the vice, yanking his nephew's arm in the process. Before Soapy could complain, Finn slammed the white seat downwards with his full strength. Soapy watched as it simply bounced off the heavy vice and whacked him full in the face. He went spinning backwards and landed on Soapy's dad, winding him with a loud, "Oof!" The toilet seat was undamaged.

As the two bruised men stood up, Soapy watched a trickle of blood roll down his uncle's nose and onto his shirt. The garage door opened. It was his mum. She half closed her eyes and sighed. "Our train is leaving in thirty-five minutes and we are going to catch it, handcuffs and spurting gashes or not."

Soapy held up his manacled wrist. "But Mum, I can't tour London with a toilet seat!"

"Yes you can, and you will. Those tickets cost £386.42 and we are not wasting them."

As usual, there was no point in arguing.

The train journey was even worse than breakfast. Soapy was given a large shopping bag to put the toilet seat in while he carried it but everyone in the carriage could clearly see that he was wearing

handcuffs and several pointed and whispered
while some people even took pictures of him on
their mobiles. His dad assured him that the family
would go to a police station right away when they
arrived and get the cuffs removed but all Soapy
could think about was who could have done this
and how. His mood wasn't helped by Topazz next
to him, giggling and making annoying comments
along the way.

"Hey, we should charge people for taking
photos – you'd make a fortune outside the Queen's
house with all the crowds," she snickered. "Get
a selfie with Toilet Boy, only five dollars."

"It's pounds here and it's not funny," muttered
Soapy.

"Come on, you gotta laugh… you Brits are
supposed to have a good
sense of humour."

"We have, but
when you're chained
to a bog seat in
public you tend
to lose it."

"Hey, don't get
worked up, Soapy,

you're looking a bit hot – flushed, you might say."

At this point Aunt Dove, who had tried her best to be sympathetic during the journey, let out a rude snort. "Topazz, honey, that was such a neat joke."

Uncle Finn, a large plaster over the bridge of his nose, couldn't resist joining in.

"Yeah, look on the bright side, kiddo, if you need a pee in London you can go any time!"

Topazz wiped her eyes. "Hey, don't call him Pugh any more, from now on it's 'Lou': 'Lou Seat'."

At this point all three bent over and guffawed so loudly that some passengers stood up to see what was going on.

And at that precise moment, Soapy knew who it was.

Loo... Of course! And there was custard too.

They were just the things they had been talking about last night in the restaurant and exactly the things he was pranked with. It was way too much of a coincidence. *But what about the Fun Snaps in the bathroom? Of course – 'bangs'!* Topazz had pulled a face when he laughed at the word...

There was no doubt about it.

It was her.

7
The finger is pointed

As soon as they left the train at King's Cross Station, Soapy headed for his mum who was marching down the crowded platform already looking for a police officer to help them unlock the handcuffs. He thought that she would be able to prove him right; she was a lawyer, after all, and all of the evidence was there.

"Mum, wait – I can't walk fast with this stupid toilet seat."

She barely turned to look. "Well you shouldn't have chained yourself to it, should you?"

"I told you, Mum – it wasn't me! Why would I prank myself? Anyway, I know who did it – I've found out."

At this point she stopped abruptly, causing at least nine people to crash into the back of the American relatives behind her.

"Oh yes, who was it, then?" She didn't keep her voice down at all.

Soapy gulped and turned to his cousin. He raised his arm and pointed, forgetting that it was still chained to the lav seat, which lifted out of the bag. A man on the platform opposite saw it, staring so hard that he walked straight into an open train door.

"It was her."

"Topazz?" shrilled his mother. Topazz's jaw dropped open in bewilderment. "What on earth makes you think it was her?"

Soapy was instantly aware that he was surrounded by five angry people. "Well, we were talking about, er, toilets at the meal last night and we mentioned custard too and bangs and that's what I was pranked with and, er, well, Topazz, she pulled a face in the restaurant and…"

Soapy's mum glared at her son and raised her voice even further. "Pugh Thompson, I have never heard such utter nonsense in my life. You're in danger of spoiling our visitors' holiday by accusing them of such things!"

Soapy just stood, speechless. He thought she'd believe him.

Uncle Finn turned to Topazz. "Well, let's see what she has to say. Look at me young lady and tell the truth. Did you do this to your cousin?"

Topazz's mouth was tight and Soapy could see a dangerous fire in her eyes. She almost spat out the words. "No I did not! He's lying. How could I have done it? I admit I like pranks but I wouldn't know how to remove a toilet seat. And where did I get handcuffs in the middle of the night? If I'd bought them from home they would have been detected at airport security. And I've never even heard of those snap things." Her chest was rising and falling as she spoke.

Aunt Dove put a hand on her shoulder. "She has a point. There's no way you can bring something like metal handcuffs through an airport now. And I presume you don't keep a set in your house?"

It was Dad's turn to speak. "No we don't. You're right and I think Topazz is telling the truth too." All of the adults nodded. "It's a ridiculous thing to accuse her of."

Soapy felt squashed, like a beetle that had been half-trodden on. "Well someone did it," he managed to mumble.

His mum took over again. "Oh yes, we can all see that someone did it and I think you know who really did it, too. But to accuse Topazz... Even if she had wanted to pull off this idiotic practical joke and had miraculously assembled all of the components, how on earth would she have managed to lock a pair of handcuffs on you while you were sleeping, hmm?"

There followed a brief silence before Soapy heard a quiet sobbing.

Topazz had buried her face into her mum's shoulder and was blubbering, "I didn't do it Mum, honestly. I swear on the Bible that I didn't have anything to do with it."

Dove stroked the back of her silky hair and whispered, "Of course you didn't, honey. Don't worry, no one believes him."

Dad suddenly clapped his hands. "Right, come on. We're not letting this silly episode ruin our trip to London. Let's get these handcuffs sorted and then see some sights and have some fun. Topazz, we'll treat you to something really special."

Soapy sat in the small police room feeling as miserable as he'd ever felt. The sign above said 'King's Cross', which didn't surprise him because everyone else was cross and it was all his fault apparently. He had been the victim, the one who'd been pranked but no one seemed to care about that and now he was being blamed for ruining the day out.

Even worse, if it wasn't Topazz then he still didn't know who had done it – they could easily strike again.

It didn't help when a policeman finally appeared and looked at the handcuffs.

"Oh, dear, prankster in the family, eh? Quite comical that."

"Yes, but what about unlocking the handcuffs, officer?" said Soapy's mum, trying but failing to be patient.

"Oh, we don't use this sort. Our keys won't work. Nothing I can do, sorry – your best bet is a locksmith."

The locksmith, who they found after searching for nearly an hour, charged £149 to remove the handcuffs, which put Soapy's parents in an even worse mood. What is more, as Soapy sat there while the locksmith fiddled with various keys, he glanced up and caught Topazz's eye. There was no mistaking the words she mouthed at him silently.

"I am going to get you."

It looked like their brief friendship was over.

8
Smelicatessen

Soapy trailed round behind everyone as they walked the heaving streets of the capital, not even able to enjoy the fact that the handcuffs and seat were now gone. There was a sore bruise on his wrist and he wished he were back home with Arvo and Loogi so they could help him solve the mystery. To make things worse, he now had an enemy staying at his house and out to gain revenge.

After a dreary hour watching the Changing of the Guards and a mope around Madame Tussauds, at last Dad announced they could have afternoon tea in Harrods. As with everything else in London, they had to queue first.

"This is boring," grumbled Topazz to her mum. "I thought the whole English queuing thing was a joke but it turns out it's true."

Aunt Dove gave her a cuddle and tried to be positive. "Hey, but it's going to be delicious. While you're waiting you can do some celebrity-spotting. This is the poshest shop around so we're bound to see Hugh Grant in a moment. Has that headache you had gone now, sweetie?"

Soapy stopped listening and instead let his imagination replace it with a silly conversation.

Topazz:	*Hey, mum is that Prince Harry?*
Dove:	*Yes, sugar.*
Topazz:	*Is he related to Harry Potter?*
Dove:	*No, no, no, Harry Potter is related to David Beckham.*
Topazz:	*Who is David Beckham?*
Dove:	*He's the British Prime Minister, honey – everyone knows that.*
Topazz:	*Have you seen Keira Knightley?*
Dove:	*No, just once.*
Topazz:	*Oh, wow, look there's Doctor Who!*
Dove:	*No, silly, that's Benedict Cucumberpatch.*

Both families stuffed themselves full of fancy sandwiches and cakes for afternoon tea and it finally seemed that everyone was cheering up.

"Well, that was de-hyper-licious," said Finn rubbing his bulging stomach.

"Amazing," said Topazz and Dove, nodding.

Soapy's dad looked hugely relieved that at last something had gone right. "What would you like to do next?" he asked.

Finn pointed across to the huge Harrods Food Halls. "Well, I want to buy a few tasty goodies to take back to the States for presents."

"Ooh, great idea," said Dove.

The bill arrived and Soapy's mum grabbed it. He saw her eyes grow huge. After this Soapy wandered round with his dad while the other four looked at hampers. "Dad, I need the loo," he said, seeing an opportunity.

"OK, I'll stay here," said his father, who was clearly trying to avoid spending any more money.

Soapy skipped into the gents and locked himself in a cubicle. Like everything else it was fancy and reeked of peculiar scent. (Soapy had a particularly acute sense of smell). He sat on the loo, glad that he was no longer chained to one, and reached for his mobile phone. A moment later Loogi was on the line.

"Hey, what's up Soapy? And what's down too?"

"It's good to hear you, Loogs. *I'm* down really. What a day…"

"Hang there, I'll go and get Arvo."

Three minutes later Soapy had explained the whole handcuff episode including Topazz's strong denial. "So, it's another prank mystery and I need your help to solve it."

Arvo now spoke. "I am seeing, this is indeed most strange. All the clues are pointing to this cousin yet she really looked shocked when you did the accuse?"

"That's right – she even swore on the Bible that it wasn't her. Her parents believe her too."

"But it is suspicious, for sure," said Loogi. "Especial when she made the threat to get you."

"Yeah, but that may be just because she's mad that I blamed her when she didn't do it."

"Truth," said Loogi, "But this puzzle must be solved and the prankster of sneak must be stopped before your whole Easter hols become the ruin."

Arvo came back on. "And we will assist you again."

"Thanks you two – I knew you'd help."

"But one thing," added Arvo. "You are sure as the

big sure that this was not Prankenstein himself?"

"I'm not sure of anything anymore," sighed Soapy.

When he returned from the loo, Soapy noticed
that his father was sitting and looking at his phone.
Soapy was about to return to him when a big sign
caught his eye: 'Harrods Famous Delicatessen'.
He wasn't completely sure what a delicatessen
was but it stank so much that he thought it should
be called a smelicatessen. He had a look inside
and discovered the origin of the mighty pong:
a giant counter of whiffy cheese. There were at
least 200 types.

Ugh!

He was about to leave when something else
caught his eye further along the enormous glass
counter. They were small and brown and curiously
speckled. He went to take a closer look. 'Quail eggs'
said a label. He'd never seen such mini eggs.
What use are they for dipping soldiers in?

And then an idea popped into his head.

Eggs.

Topazz.

Allergic.

She said that she was going to get him. Well

what if he armed himself with something powerful first? Something small that he could sneak into a pocket? Something that might just scare her off? He looked back and saw no sign of Dad looking his way. The eggs were £1 each but it was worth it. He bought two and had them carefully wrapped before they were put in the shopping bag.

Soapy was right that his dad hadn't seen him but what he didn't know was that someone else had – someone tanned with long blonde hair.

Topazz realised right away what Soapy was up to. Why else would he buy just two tiny eggs?

Her mum was busy talking to Soapy's mum and hadn't noticed what was going on. Topazz saw her chance.

"Mum, can I go over there to the counter and buy some olives or something?"

Dove gave her a smile. "Sure, sugar – just don't wander anywhere else. We'll be here."

Topazz went over to the olives then moved further down the counter, checking that no one was watching her. The smell here was stupendous. She gave one last glance back then saw her chance.

"Can I get that piece of Manchego cheese just there please?"

9
Weapons of mass pranking

That evening, back at his house, Soapy hid the two tiny eggs in his money box and placed it in a secret compartment he'd made behind his bookshelf. He then considered how he should best deploy his new eggy weapon.

Just an hour later, when everyone was in bed, Topazz crept out of her room and snuck down the stairs. She found a plastic container with a tight lid in the kitchen, placed the Manchego cheese inside and pushed it right to the back of the gloomy cupboard she had spotted earlier under the stairs, behind Ivette's vacuum cleaner and a stack of old shoes. It was primed and ready to go off whenever she needed it.

The following day the Thompsons' visitors said they just wanted to rest and relax and so no activities

were planned. By mid-morning
Soapy was bored. He'd read one
of his library books and played a
couple of console games but what
he really wanted to do was to see
his friends so they could start
their prank detective operation.
He found his mum in her study.

"Mum, can Arvo and Loogi
come round?"

"Certainly not. We've got
visitors already and anyway,
you don't deserve it after what
you did to Topazz yesterday."

He was going to protest his
innocence once more but changed his mind.

"Well, can I go round to theirs?"

"Look, I am trying to work. We have to pay
for that obscenely expensive day in London. You
know you don't deserve to see your friends so stop
asking. Just go to your room and be quiet."

Back in his bedroom, Soapy tried calling Arvo
and Loogi but they didn't answer. He decided that
he would have to begin solving the handcuff and

custard mystery himself. He sat down and started to think.

Well, at least no more pranks happened last night so that's a start.

After coming up with no ideas at all he did a quick online search for how to solve crimes and discovered that a good way to start is to find out who has a motive.

What is a motive? Something to do with cars? Maybe a motive is a tool for breaking into houses, like a crowbar. Perhaps all serious pranksters own a set of these motives. Prankenstein must have loads stashed somewhere.

He checked a dictionary to be sure.

motive (noun) a reason for doing something

Ah. Not a crowbar then. But who would have a reason for pranking him? Someone who didn't like him? Chinny, his teacher last year? He couldn't imagine him going for a toilet seat gag. Venus Bray, the girl who'd bullied him for years? Would she have broken into his house in the night with custard? Unlikely. What about all of the victims of Prankenstein? But the whole point was that nobody knew he was Prankenstein except for Arvo and Loogi and they were his best friends.

Perhaps thinking of the motive was the wrong approach. Maybe he needed to look at the prank itself. It would need to be someone daring with a crazy sense of humour, good at handling dessert sauces... Someone sneaky who could slip handcuffs onto a sleeping boy too... Someone clever enough to know that he'd go to the bathroom and set off the Fun Snaps...

Wow, this is quite a villain.

Then an idea popped into his head: *Fingerprints!* The culprit must have left them on lots of surfaces. He looked on his bed frame and couldn't see anything. *How do you see fingerprints?* He was about to look on the internet when a thought crossed his mind. His bedroom would be full of everyone's fingerprints, and the bathroom too – his, Dad's, Mum's, Ivette's, Topazz's...

Topazz. Could it have been her? Something at the back of his mind kept returning to that conversation in the restaurant. Loos, custard, bangs. *But what was her motive?* He mulled it over for another minute before a quiet knock at the door broke his concentration.

Intrigued, he turned the handle.
It was Topazz.

They looked at each other for a moment, unsure what to say. Then she spoke in a subdued voice.
"Can I come in?"
Soapy wasn't sure if he wanted to speak to her but perhaps she had some information on who the prankster might be. He opened the door further and she walked inside.

"I thought you were going to get me," he said.

"Look, Soapy, you gotta believe me. It wasn't me – it really wasn't. I swear, truly, truly. Why would I prank you? I like you, you know that, even though you accused me in front of everyone yesterday."

"Then why are you here if I did such a bad thing?"

"Well, because I would have done the same in your place. I've thought about it. The whole thing is really weird and it's no surprise that you would blame a visitor like that – especially as I told you I like pranks."

Soapy spread his palms. "Somebody did it and I just don't know who."

Topazz nodded. "I know, I know. I want to help you find out who it was. But you must believe me that I just wouldn't know how to do a bunch of nuts stuff like that – I don't own handcuffs. And I really don't carry custard around with me."

She stood with her arms out and looked into his eyes. Something inside Soapy told him that she was telling the truth.

"OK," he half croaked. "I'm, I'm sorry for accusing you. I was just mad about it and I needed someone to blame."

"Hey, no worries. I don't want us to be not

speaking while I'm here.
I want to be friends – it'll
be more fun. I've asked
if tomorrow we can go
to Alton Towers. My
dad has offered to pay.
How does that sound?"

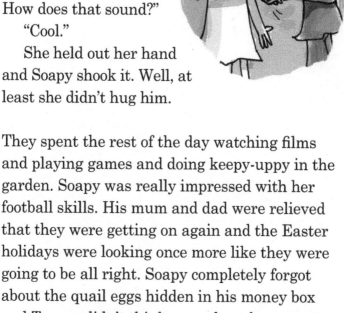

"Cool."

She held out her hand
and Soapy shook it. Well, at
least she didn't hug him.

They spent the rest of the day watching films
and playing games and doing keepy-uppy in the
garden. Soapy was really impressed with her
football skills. His mum and dad were relieved
that they were getting on again and the Easter
holidays were looking once more like they were
going to be all right. Soapy completely forgot
about the quail eggs hidden in his money box
and Topazz didn't think once about her secret
stash of Manchego cheese. She was also feeling
much better after the headache that she had
woken with again had finally gone.

At bedtime Soapy texted Arvo and Loogi to

say that peace was restored with the Americans. He climbed into bed and read a chapter of 'The Hobbit' then switched off his light. As he yawned, some little brain-reminder cell pinged and he realised that he hadn't taken his red anti-sleepwalking pill. Soapy reached for his bedside drawer and pulled out the small plastic bottle of pills, popping one on his tongue then swallowing a gulp of water to wash it down. His eyes were closed the whole time but even if they had been open, he wouldn't have seen the empty vitamin tablet bottle under his bed or noticed the scatter of small red pills amongst the bushes outside beneath his window.

10
Hairy cousin

Topazz awoke the following morning feeling strangely itchy. Her whole head felt kind of tickly and different. She sat up and scratched her long hair.

It wasn't there.

Well, some of it was there but for some reason it felt short. She thought that she must be imagining it, so she slipped out of bed and started walking

to the mirror on the wall opposite. Somehow her lower face was prickly in a way that she'd never felt before. She rubbed her fingers over her chin and was disturbed that it felt hairy. The mirror explained everything.

She had a beard.

A scruffy, blonde beard. Topazz turned her head. Her beautiful long silky hair was gone. In its place she had just short ugly tufts – the rest was somehow stuck to her chin.

It must be a dream. Then a small object on the floor caught her eye, a tube of glue. Near it was a large pair of kitchen scissors. It was not a dream.

She screamed.

The piercing sound was of almost military power. The whole house trembled and within moments every person in it came running to see what had happened.

Soapy was the last to arrive; he would have been quicker if he hadn't been slowed down by a pounding headache.

Soapy watched in horror as Topazz jiggled and shrieked and pulled at the long strands of fair hair glued to her chin while her mum fretted around her and her dad tried to calm her down. Soapy's mum and dad looked at her with dismay and then turned to their son who was cowering in the corner in anticipation. Their eyes were burning with fury.

"I know it's hardly worth me saying," he whimpered. "But it wasn't me."

His dad pointed to the door and growled, "Back to your room, now!"

As Soapy slunk away he heard his mum mutter, "That boy is determined to ruin their stay..."

Soapy's mind did its best to become alert as he trudged back to his bedroom.

What was going on? Just a few hours ago he and Topazz were friends again and everything looked like it was back to normal. *How could this have happened?* The headache continued to batter at his skull, muddying his thoughts. But then his brain began to make connections.

The headache.

A nasty prank.

That meant one thing: Prankenstein.

But he only turned into Prankenstein when he sleepwalked and ate cheese. He couldn't have been sleepwalking because he'd taken a tablet – he remembered it distinctly. Soapy opened his bedside drawer to check the tablets. The brown plastic bottle was there and there were eight or nine red pills inside. They looked a bit different from what he'd remembered, but then he couldn't be sure what they did look like.

It must be something else.

Maybe the Americans had brought some cheese into the house by accident?

Soapy opened his door and stuck his head out. He could hear the four adults in Topazz's room trying to calm her down and discussing how to remove the beard. He caught snippets of the conversation.

"We are so, so sorry."

"We could try pulling it off."

"No one else here has woken up with a beard."

"You'll have to shave."

They could be there for some time. Soapy decided to risk it. He skipped out onto the landing and tumbled down the stairs and into the kitchen. He opened food cupboards and then the fridge.

No sign of cheese anywhere.

He checked a couple of plastic containers and a half-squashed white cardboard box but that just contained a few

crumbs of what looked like cake. No cheese anywhere. He scooted back upstairs before he was discovered.

Well if it wasn't Prankenstein who on earth was it? Dove or Finn wouldn't prank their own daughter. He gave Arvo and Loogi a quick call.

"Arvo, are you both at home today? I really need to see you urgently."

"Yes, why this is?"

"I can't tell you now but I am in BIG trouble."

"Otch. Can you come round to our house to do the telling?"

"I don't think I'll be allowed somehow. I'll have to go, someone is coming." Soapy quickly hid his phone as he heard footsteps on the landing.

The door flew open and his mother marched in followed by his father. Each had huffing nostrils and fierce eyes.

"Pugh, we need to know the truth here and now," she said. "This is getting out of hand. Did you cut off Topazz's hair last night?"

He looked at them as calmly as he could. "No, Mum. Honestly, it wasn't me." Soapy's dad looked at him intently. "Do you promise because if we find out it was you then you will regret it for a very long time."

He shook his head. "I promise it wasn't me. I like Topazz. I wouldn't do that to her."

His mum's mouth was tight and pale. "Well it doesn't look good, does it? You accuse someone of playing a prank on you and then very soon afterwards a horrible, mean prank is played on her. In a court of law you'd be halfway to prison."

"But Mum, I said it honestly wasn't me and it wasn't."

They looked at him for a moment. He didn't turn away.

Dad spoke first. "I know this is odd, but I believe him."

Soapy almost fell off his bed when his mum said, "Astonishingly, in the circumstances, so do I."

"Well who was it then?" said Dad, throwing his arms in the air. "This is just like last year when we had that cow in the house and someone dyed my face green."

"And stuck my bottom to a stool," added Mum.

Soapy said nothing.

"The problem is," continued Dad, "Finn, Dove and Topazz are convinced that Soapy is responsible. What are we going to do about that?"

Mum put her fingers
to her lips and pondered.
"I think it might be
best if we kept the
two children properly
apart for a while."

"I could take
Soapy to the golf
club or the restaurant,
maybe," suggested Dad.

Soapy raised a finger.
"Would it save you the
trouble if I spent the
day at Arvo and
Loogi's house? They said I could."

His parents looked at each other and Mum
nodded. "That's probably a good idea."

She was about to go and call the Twince's
parents when she noticed the medicine bottle of
sleepwalking pills next to Soapy's bed.

"You have been taking one every night, haven't
you?" she said, looking at him then picking up
the bottle.

"Yes, I haven't done any sleepwalking at all."

"Just as well," said Dad.

Mum rattled the bottle. "Not very many left – I'll top this up." She left the room and returned a minute later with a large plastic tub of red tablets, emptying twenty or thirty into Soapy's bottle. "It's a good job these are harmless," she said.

Half an hour later, Soapy was in his mum's car for the short drive across town to Arvo and Loogi's house. He'd set his mobile to silent but felt it vibrate. Quietly he slipped it out of his pocket. There was a text. It was from Topazz.

THIS TIME I REALLY AM GOING TO GET YOU.

11
Pant revenge

The Twince's house was very different to Soapy's.
For a start, it was a tall, narrow terraced house
in the old part of town by the river. Soapy's house
was new, on a quiet outlying estate and inside
it was modern, always tidy and very clean. Arvo
and Loogi's house was none of these things. It was
chaotic and cluttered and full of strange objects
piled up in the high-ceilinged
rooms. Soapy loved it.

He also liked the
brothers' parents who
mainly worked at home.
They were both from
Estonia and had moved
to the UK a few years
previously. Pinja was
the Twince's mum. She

was a quiet, bespectacled photographer who specialised in pictures of bare feet. She had once asked if she could look at Soapy's feet but declared them 'too boring and normal'. She said she liked interesting feet with twists and bumps, lumpy veins and long hairy toes. "Old people have the best foot far by," she'd once said.

The boys' dad was called Olof. He was small with fiery red hair and mangled clothes. He worked in the large basement of the house and he was an artist of sorts, a kind of zany sculptor. His speciality was what he called 'fused objects' (although Arvo called them confused objects). Soapy loved these – they were mixtures of two everyday items, cunningly combined so that they looked like they could really work: a toaster and spade, a chair and lawnmower or a vacuum cleaner and skateboard. Soapy's favourite was the motorcycle bath that Olof had sold to a New York gallery for 12,000 dollars much to his delight. Most of his other creations cluttered the house, driving everyone mad.

Arvo and Loogi each had their own room on the third floor of the house. Arvo's was full of boxes of animal bones that he'd collected on walks and via web auctions. He called them 'bonce' which never failed to make Soapy laugh.

Loogi's room was more orderly with everything neatly filed in drawers and cupboards. His passion was solving puzzles and he had shelves full of crossword books and piles of puzzle magazines all in date order.

The Twince also had a baby brother called Mikk who, although friendly and loveable, had an unpleasant habit of vomiting on anyone who picked him up. His nickname was Sick Mikk. Soapy tended to steer clear of him.

The three friends spent the morning in Arvo's room discussing the strange events of the previous few days. Soapy brought them up to date regarding the beard prank and when he told them about Topazz's fuming text their eyes were wide.

"Wow, that girl is madly hopping," said Arvo.

"Hopping mad, you mean," corrected Loogi.

"Whatever," said Soapy. "The main thing is we've got to find out who's doing all these pranks at my house before something really terrible happens. It's bad enough as it is."

"Of course," announced Arvo. "We will do the

solving. After all, we made discovery the true identity of Prankenstein the last time."

Loogi held up a finger. "First, most important, we must be deciding on our detective approach."

"What do you mean?" said Soapy.

"Well," said Arvo, "we have been thinking on this. The last big pranking occasion we were basing our investigations on was the model of Shylock Holmes and Doctor Watnot."

Loogi nodded. "That was suitable oldy Victorian sleuth duo for the Doctor Jackal and Mr Hyde mystery of your transformations."

Soapy shrugged. "You two have me really confused."

"No, this is very forwardstraight, Soapy," said Arvo, twiddling with a vole spine. "With these American cousins involved this time we brothers are using the more modern TV detecting model. We thought maybe Starkers and Hunch."

"Who, what?"

"You know, those underblanket US cops who are jumping on the cars."

"Oh, you mean Starsky and Hutch? My dad watched those when he was a kid – they're ancient," laughed Soapy.

Loogi twisted his lip. "Ah true. What about then Cockney and Lazy?"

"Cagney and Lacey? They're also from the Stone Age."

Arvo looked for a piece of paper. "Who were those other ones, who did the biffing of aliens? Er, Murder and Scally, or something."

"Mulder and Scully – 'The X-Files'," said Soapy. "Yeah, that's more like it."

Loogi twisted his nose. "Or would classic old-school English solver be best? Who was guy

with Jag and grump? Morph and Lewisham?"

Soapy smiled. "Morse and Lewis. Now you're onto stuff my mum likes."

An hour later they had given up the idea of copying TV detectives and were wondering what to do about Topazz's threat.

"She's going to do something terrible to me tonight, I know it," said Soapy.

"Why don't you do asking to spend the night here?" said Loogi. "Then you have more safety."

Arvo nodded. "It is school holidays. That is top plan."

The conversation was interrupted by footsteps on the stairs. Pinja then appeared carrying a tray of drinks and turquoise biscuits. Arvo gabbled something at her in Estonian.

"Speak of the English, so Zoapy can be following," she said.

Loogi sighed. "Mother, can our friend be staying the night?"

"Of course, if he has the allowance of parents. He will have need of toothbrush."

"I'll call them now," said Soapy, pulling out his mobile.

Pinja's smoke-blowing VW camper van parped and rattled back to Soapy's house with the three boys on board. Soapy wondered if he'd see Topazz or his aunt and uncle while he nipped inside to pick up some overnight things and a change of clothes. There was no sign of them as he scuttled up the stairs. His mother had probably wisely kept them in another part of the house.

Soapy pushed open his bedroom door and froze. There were clothes scattered all over the carpet. His wardrobe was wide open and all of his drawers too. He picked up a pair of jeans and then noticed that all of the items scattered across the floor were either trousers, shorts or underpants. Then he noticed something else. The jeans had a large hole cut into the seat. They were his best pair too.

He grabbed another pair – some navy school trousers – and discovered that they too had a huge rough hole in the bum area. He picked up some shorts: the same thing. Then he noticed lots of ragged scraps of material lying amongst the clothes and the same pair of scissors that Topazz had found in her room. Every single item had a gaping space cut in the back, even the undies.

His bottom was going to be on display an awful lot. Soapy gulped and dropped onto his bed.

It has started.

This is like war.

Then he saw a scrap of paper on his bed. There was writing on it.

Soapy was just thinking that at least he had the trousers he was wearing when something else on the floor caught his eye between the piles of ruined pants on the floor. It was a small lid from the box in which he kept his bee collection. But where was the rest of it? He dug around through the clothes and looked in all of his cupboards but it was gone.

He rushed to the bathroom and found the rest of the box there, empty.

But why the bathroom?

And then he realised: Topazz had flushed his bees down the toilet.

Soapy stood for a moment, his heart pounding, unsure whether to tell his parents what had happened. If I do, then there'll be another huge inquest and I won't be able to go back to the Twince.

He returned to his bedroom and shoved all of the vandalised clothes into his wardrobe, pocketed the note, closed everything up then hurried out to Pinja's car carrying his toothbrush, a red tablet, some pyjamas and a pair of highly ventilated pants.

12
Puzzles and plans

Back inside Arvo's bedroom, Soapy was livid.

"That's it, she's done it now – she's killed my bees!"

Loogi frowned. "But they were already being dead."

"That's not the point. It took me ages to collect all those bees. There were nine different types and that spiteful American kid has flushed them down the sewer."

Arvo held up his hands. "Hey Soapy, you need to do the calming. You almost shout."

Soapy's face was sizzling. "I will not calm down. She has cut holes in all of my trousers – my mum won't buy me any more because she'll say it's my fault. I'm going to be spending Easter with my backside hanging out and the whole town laughing at me."

"Hmmm, that is not the ideal," mumbled Loogi.

"Well she's gone too far now," growled Soapy, his teeth grinding slowly. "She's going to get what she deserves."

Arvo glanced at his brother. "What are you meaning?"

"Get me some cheese. I am going to unleash Prankenstein."

It took the Twince nearly the rest of the morning to convince their friend that this was far too dangerous a move.

"He is the uncontrollable one, Soapy."

"He could do *anything!*"

"He might be getting Topazz but he will also do the big prank on others – your family, your aunt and uncle, your neighbours, the school teachers. Recall the last time. He might even be pranking us again."

Soapy came to

his senses. "You're right. I wouldn't want that to happen. You're the only real friends I have in all this."

Arvo nodded. "And we have been keeping your secret secret."

He looked at the brothers. "Yes, I'm really grateful for that. OK, Prankenstein won't be recalled for now – but what are we going to do?"

Loogi had been deep in thought. He now looked up. "We must be solving the puzzle. We must be studying the clues. We must be finding the evidences, and…"

Soapy waited. "And what?"

"I have already been doing much of this and I have the bad-bad feeling."

"I too," murmured Arvo.

"What?" Soapy's mouth was open.

"That Prankenstein is already on loose."

After a hasty lunch of slimy mackerel, red cabbage and indestructible bread, the three boys sat down upstairs once more with sheets of paper and began to write down all of the details of the peculiar happenings so far. Loogi labelled the pages and arranged everything in a logical order.

Eventually they had this:

Prank 1: Handcuffs
- S handcuffed to toilet seat
- Custard in slippers
- Bangers in bathroom
- 2 families talking about these beforehand
- T says she did not do it.

Prank 2: Beard
- T has hair cut off
- She has glue beard
- T thinks S did this
- S had headache

Prank 3: Trousers
- Holes cut in pants
- Bees down the loo
- T says she did this (leaves note)

Main suspect: Topazz
- American
- Allergic to eggs
- Likes pranks
- Admits to one prank but not other

They studied the scraps of paper for a while.

"Are you sure there is nothing more you can be telling us?" Loogi asked Soapy.

He thought hard. "The strange thing is, she admitted that she did the trouser prank but she swears that she didn't do the handcuff one."

Arvo scratched his head. "Hmmm, that is most interest. Was there anything different about her each time?"

Soapy tried to replay the events in his mind. "Yes, hang on. I remember now – she complained about headaches the day I was pranked with the toilet seat."

Loogi's eyes lit up. "Ah! This could be the vital." He scribbled it down on paper.

"And you had the headache too this morning?" asked Arvo.

"Yes," said Soapy. "I know what you're thinking. Every time I eat cheese and turn into Prankenstein in the night I get a headache next morning – but I had a pill to stop me sleepwalking and there's no cheese in the house."

Loogi put a finger up. "Yes, but the pranky beast could be hiding cheese like last time. Although that is not explaining the sleepwalk."

At that moment, the three boys heard footsteps approaching up the stairs. Arvo grabbed the sheets of paper and shoved them up his jumper a second before the door swung open and Pinja, the Twince's mum appeared. She was holding a phone.

"Zoapy, this is your mother being on the call. She says she is taking visitors to see the granny tomorrow of the morning and can you be staying here for the lunch then because Ivette is away? This by me is OK."

Soapy looked at the Twince and nodded. He was happy to stay away from the prank mania

that had enveloped his home.

Pinja then turned to Arvo. "Are you having the windy illness? Your belly is shape of gripe."

"No, no," he said, trying to cover the lumps. "I am possessing health perfection."

She looked doubtful but turned back down the stairs, putting the phone to her ear. "Yes, Zoapy is glad to stay and we are having plenty of pickly vinegar mackerel to feed him."

They waited until the footsteps died away then all breathed a sigh of relief.

"Hey," said Loogi, "this is news tremendous."

Soapy grimaced. "It's not that good – I hate that manky fish."

"No, no – are you not seeing?"

"What, brother?" said Arvo.

There was a glint in Loogi's eye. "Tomorrow morning, Soapy's parents and the Americans are at house of granny and Ivette is gone too."

"So?" said Soapy.

"Your house is being empty. We can sneak in and do the search for clues."

13
The chicken and the egg

Soapy awoke at the Twince's house after a blissfully
uneventful night. There was no headache and no
sign that he had been savagely pranked in any
way. During a daunting breakfast of black pudding
and porridge cakes served up by Olof, Arvo put
the first part of the boys' daring plan into action.

"Father, is it being OK if we are playing in the
park after this?"

"Well, if you are stuck together it is right, I am
supposing."

Loogi added, "There are being three of us and
we have phones."

Olof nodded. "OK, just back here twelve, yes?"

They thanked him and slipped out of the
kitchen, quickly putting on their shoes and coats
before scuttling through the front door.

"That's amazing, my parents would never let

me go out like that without an adult and possibly two bodyguards with Alsatians," cackled Soapy.

"We must be hurrying though if we are to make of the search your house," said Arvo.

Soapy looked at him with admiration. "I was amazed at how coolly you lied there about going to the park."

Loogi tapped his head. "It was no lie, to the park we go now."

"But I thought we were going to sneak into my house?"

Arvo gave a sly chuckle then winked. "Park two minutes, house two hours."

"Ooh, clever..." said Soapy. "Nobody said we *couldn't* go to my house."

"Exact," said Loogi, extracting a Sudoku as they trotted down the road.

Soapy felt very strange approaching his house in such underhand circumstances. The three boys sidled along hedges and peeped between fences trying to get a glimpse of the driveway to check which cars were there. They hid behind a van parked next door and Arvo peered through the cab windows.

"There is silver car in drive but that is all. No lights being on in house."

"That's my dad's car," said Soapy. They'll have gone to granny's in my mum's – it's more comfortable."

"But how can we be total sure they are all out?" said Arvo.

Loogi whispered, "I am having idea. We knock on door and do the scarper. See if door is answered."

"Nice one," said Soapy. "You go."

Loogi shook his head. "I am thinking you are fastest runner. Speedy king."

Soapy pouted. "I can't do knock-a-door-run on my own house, that's…"

"… chance in lifetime," said Arvo.

"You always craved the pranking – now is perfect."

He admitted they were right and, feeling highly shady, snuck along to the front door, pushing the doorbell hard then careering back to the cover of the van, panting like a spaniel.

They watched.

No one answered the door.

The boys high-fived each other, Soapy produced his back door key and a minute later they were inside his house, feeling almost like burglars.

Arvo took command. "Right, work good so far, detectors. Now we must split and make the clue search. I will go to the room of Topazz, Loogi you do looking downstairs and Soapy the rest of the up, OK? Meeting back here in thirty minutes."

Soapy decided to check his room first. It appeared to be just as he'd left it the day before, with no indication that anyone had discovered the ruined trouser stash. He checked the cupboards, shelves and drawers carefully, not quite sure what he was looking for. Nothing was unusual.

He tried under his bed next and saw a small white plastic pot. Bringing it out he read the label:

MULTI-VITAMINS
TAKE ONE A DAY TO KEEP
THE DOC AT BAY

Hmmm, not mine. More like the kind of thing that Dad takes.

He popped it in his pocket then went to check his secret hiding place behind his books. The money box was there but it felt suspiciously light. He checked the lock. It was open. What's more, the box was empty.

Soapy ran downstairs to tell the other two. Loogi was waiting but Arvo was still upstairs. He appeared when he heard their voices.

"Look," said Soapy holding out the box, "This is where I hid the quail eggs – they're gone. Topazz must have taken them but it doesn't make sense because she's allergic to eggs. Oh, and I found this empty vitamin pill bottle under my bed."

"Interesting, most," said Arvo. "Did you make any discovery, Loogi?"

He shrugged. "No things much unusual downstairs – just the cupboard here with stinky whiff." He opened the small door under the stairs and the boys agreed that it did have a most peculiar pong inside, although they couldn't find what was causing it.

"That stench is kind of familiar," said Soapy, twitching his nose. "Dunno where from, though. Anyway, what did you find in Topazz's room, Arvo?"

From behind his back he produced two objects.

"One small key, perhaps being from money box, I am thinking. And one small book."

Soapy picked up the key. "That *is* from my money box. So she did take the eggs! This really doesn't make sense.... What's the book?"

Arvo smiled, clearly pleased with himself. "Ah, that most interesting of all."

Loogi looked at him. "Well?"

"It is being a diary. The diary of Topazz."

The boys stood and looked at the slim, gold-rimmed journal for several moments before anyone said anything. Here was something both invaluable and dangerous. Very dangerous.

"Have you done the reading of it?" asked Loogi.

Arvo shook his head. "No. I thought Soapy would be the one to extract the most sense from this."

"Me?" Soapy screeched. "I am not reading her diary. Imagine if she found out! Reading a girl's diary is second only to genocide as the most grievous crime on the planet – everyone knows that."

Loogi held out a hand. "Here, I will do the study of this. You two of the wimp kind go outside and do the garden search for more clues."

They didn't argue.

Outside, examining the shed, bushes and plants brought back memories of the desperate search for the small parcels of Stilton that Prankenstein had stashed all over the garden the previous year. Soapy found nothing in the shed this time and the only unusual things he saw were some odd red patches on the soil underneath his window. He called Arvo over to look at them.

"Hmmm, these are mystery – unless your flower bed is developing the pimples."

"Did you find anything in the rest of the garden?" said Soapy.

"No, except that I am hearing noises of the eerie kind up by the fence at top."

"What kind of noises?"

"Like the scratching – like some trapped person in a cell attempting to outbreak."

Soapy's eyes went very large and the two boys tiptoed over for a closer look before a shout from the back door stopped them in their tracks. It was Loogi.

"Come quick here," he called. They ran over to see him holding open the diary. Loogi's face was pale.

Arvo held out his hands. "What is your discovery?"

Loogi opened his mouth slowly. "She sleepwalks."

"What!" cried Soapy. "She never told me that, nor did my parents."

"That is because they don't know. It's her secret."

Loogi pointed to a page of tiny handwriting.

"It says here:

Sleepwalked again last night. It's getting worse - dunno whether to tell Mum or not. Maybe that is what is giving me the headaches."

Arvo gulped. "You know what this is meaning, most of likely?"

Loogi nodded. "She did sleepwalking into Soapy's room and took the eggs."

Soapy bit his lip. "And ate them."

Arvo looked at him. "And because she has the relation to you, we can have big fear that she too has turned into prank-crazed monster."

Soapy and Arvo looked at Loogi whose voice emerged as a croak. "I've called her Yankenstein."

Once more the three friends stood silently, their mouths dry.

Yankenstein.

This explained a lot,

especially the toilet seat prank and why Topazz didn't know she'd done it. Loogi was just about to say that it didn't explain who had glued the beard on Topazz when he was interrupted by Arvo.

"Soapy, your mountain bike. Is it blue?"

"Yes."

"With black drink bottle?"

"Yes."

"And red lettering on frame?"

"Yes, why do you ask?"

He pointed. "Look up."

The other two turned to see the tall church steeple rising up behind the trees of the surrounding gardens. It usually had a weather-vane on top but now it had a shiny expensive mountain bike.

Soapy wailed. "Hey, that was a Specialized!"

Arvo shook his head. "It is very specialised now. Look,

it's even turning in the wind."

Loogi turned to the other two. "Topazz, or rather Yankenstein, doubt not. I wonder what other manky pranks she has been the doing? Were you finding anything in the garden?"

Then Arvo and Soapy remembered the scratching noises. All three of them crept up to the fence. As they approached it, a raucous call made them jump.

"Cock-a-doodle-doo!"

Then Soapy remembered. "Ah, yes, Mrs Pierce next door has chickens and a cockerel. That will explain the scratching noises."

The boys reached up and peered over the fence just to be sure. There were chickens all right and there was something else.

"Oh no," moaned Soapy.

"What? More of pranks?" said Arvo.

"No. Look next to that bush."

The Twince followed his finger and saw to their dismay four smooth, light brown ovals nestling in some long grass. Eggs. Then Arvo spotted some more.

Loogi jumped back down. "This is being a development of the serious kind. If Topazz

sleepwalks there are galore eggs for Yankenstein to be munching."

"Prank food," said Soapy, holding his head in his hands.

"Wait," said Arvo. "I just trod on object of lumpiness. Not egg." He reached down and picked up a small, reeking package wrapped in greaseproof paper.

Soapy stared in horror. There was writing all over the wrapper, repeating the same word.

'Harrods'.

Arvo opened it up, throwing his head back as the full stink met his nostrils. "Whoach, I know this, we had it on the holiday to Spanish once."

"I too," said Loogi. "Manchego cheese."

All three of them stared at the cheese and thought about what it meant. But nobody said anything.

It was almost too terrifying to contemplate. Arvo wrapped the package back up again and was just about to suggest that they flush it down the toilet when a sound stopped him in his tracks. It was a car. A car stopping nearby. Doors slammed and there were familiar voices.

"My parents!" hissed Soapy.

Adrenaline surged through the blood vessels of all three boys but none of them moved; they were all staring at the back door which was wide open. Loogi still held Topazz's diary.

There was a movement in the hallway and, without thinking, the three boys hurled themselves over the fence and into Mrs Pierce's garden. Soapy was sure that they hadn't been seen but one thing was even surer… he'd just landed on a clutch of raw eggs.

14
How to stop a monster

The boys managed to creep down the side of Mrs Pierce's house and escape out of the front garden, hidden from Soapy's house by a thick hedge. They ran all the way back to the Twince's house without stopping.

As they hurtled along, Arvo cried out, "I've still got the cheese – shall I throw it in the river?"

Soapy, barely able to breathe, shouted, "No, I might need it as evidence against Topazz. Just keep it away from me, though!"

Once safely back inside Arvo's bedroom and having made excuses for being late, the boys hid the diary and cheese then sat down and tried to make sense of everything.

"So, Topazz is doing the morph into horrid Yankenstein each night, that we can be of sure," said Loogi.

Arvo nodded. "And the cheese find is suggesting that Prankenstein is also on loose. Hence the beard prank on Topazz."

"But how?" said Soapy. "I've been taking my anti-sleepwalking pills each night."

Loogi raised a finger. "But that bottle of the vitamin – it raises suspicion."

Soapy produced it from his pocket and Arvo fired up his cranky laptop. He googled the brand of vitamin tablets on the label and discovered they were red.

"Are those looking like your medical pills?" said Arvo.

"Yes, just like them! Yankenstein must have swapped them over – that explains those red patches on the soil below my window. Those were the real pills, thrown away."

Loogi gave a heavy sigh. "So, now we have the trouble of double. Two crazed prank-playing brutes are on loose. Anything could do the happening."

"It's worse than that," said Soapy. "They are AT WAR."

After another pickled seafood lunch, Pinja announced that she'd be taking Soapy back home in half an hour. The boys raced upstairs once more, knowing that they had to think of a way to stop the two creatures before the whole town was destroyed by pranks.

"First, we must be stopping Prankenstein," said Arvo. "He is just making things the worse."

Arvo gave a nod. "Yes, it is hard problem to stop him obtaining the cheese so we must prevent sleepwalks."

"I think I can do that," said Soapy. "Mum has refilled my pill bottle, so I have plenty of proper tablets to take. I'll hide them all over my room, so even if Yankenstein nicks the bottle again, I'll have a back-up supply."

Loogi patted him on the back. "That is thinking of the excellent kind. So, we can stop Prankenstein, but how to stop the Yank version...?"

"That is harder problem," said Arvo. "There are eggs being everywhere outside."

"And now I think about it, there was Ivette's birthday cake in the fridge – that has eggs in it," said Soapy.

Loogi waggled his favourite crossword pen.

"No, the answer must be to stop her from doing the sleepwalking."

"Can you be sneaking pill into her cocoa?" said Arvo, looking at Soapy.

"That's too dangerous. And I don't think Americans have cocoa."

The ideas continued.

"Lock her in her room?"

"What if there's a fire?"

"Tie her to the bed?"

"And who is going to do *that?*"

"Stay up all night and watch her and when she sleepwalks, force pill into gob."

"I can only see about ten problems with that one…"

Then Arvo made a more serious suggestion. "Well, Soapy, you can of course be telling the parents that she does the sleepwalking. Then they will surely be giving her the tablet to fix this and presto-hey, Yankenstein is finished."

Soapy was just about to say that was a brilliant idea when something occurred to him. "But then Topazz will know that we have been reading her diary and all hell will break loose. Oh no…"

"What?" said Loogi seeing a flash of fear in

Soapy's eyes.

"The diary! We have it here – Topazz is back at my house now and she might be looking for it. I've got to sneak it back into her room somehow."

At that moment there were footsteps on the stairs again and Pinja appeared in the doorway. "Right, boys. Time to be taking Zoapy back to the home. Are you OK, Zoapy? You are looking like you have seen ghoulie."

"Er, yes, er fine. I'll just get my things." He scuttled off to find his toothbrush while Pinja picked up his pyjamas from the bed. She noticed the hole in the bottoms and held them up.

"Wows, Zoapy, that must have been trump stupendous."

Normally the boys would have laughed themselves silly at such a remark but their minds were on other things. As Soapy appeared with his washbag, Arvo nimbly slipped something into his hand so that the Twince's mother couldn't see. It was the diary.

Soapy's heart was heavy as the three boys travelled back to his house in the rattling VW camper van. To take his mind off the trouble and trauma that surely awaited him back at home

he made up an imagined comedy conversation
for his return.

Mum: *I hope you behaved yourself at your
         friends' house, Pugh.*
Soapy: *Yes, we only got up to a few little jinks,
         nothing serious.*
Dad: *Like what?*
Soapy: *Well, we pretended we were in the park
         for two hours when really we were
         breaking into someone's house.*
Mum: *What! Whose house?*
Soapy: *Ours.*
Dad: *Well, that's not so bad.*
Mum: *What exactly did
         you get up to?*
Soapy: *Nothing much
         – we just stole
         Topazz's
         diary, took a
         bottle of pills,
         discovered
         a money
         box that had
         been raided,*

broke into Mrs Pierce's garden and trod on some eggs. Oh, and found some Harrods' cheese that had been hidden under the stairs.

Dad: *Boys, eh? Used to do that sort of stuff all the time myself...*

Mum: *Well, what did you get up to at Arvo and Loogi's house?*

Soapy: *Oh, not much. We just pieced together a series of clues, identified evidence, solved several mysteries and discovered that once again on certain evenings I am transformed into a dangerous hairy prank-mad fiend.*

Dad: *Is that all? I thought it was something serious.*

Mum: *Pugh, are you telling us the whole truth?*

Soapy: *No, Mum, sorry. I admit it – there is one more thing. My American cousin is also turning into an uncontrollable big brute prank-monster called Yankenstein every night.*

Dad: *Are you sure?*

Soapy: *Yes. Oh, and the two creatures are at war.*

A sharp elbow in the ribs woke Soapy out of his dream world. It was Arvo. He was holding up his mobile phone which had a message on the screen.

When are Americans going home?
I cannot speak in case my mother
is hearing.

Soapy reached for his mobile to key in an answer but found that the battery was flat. He'd forgotten to take his charger. Loogi passed him a piece of paper and his crossword pen. Soapy wrote:

In 3 days.

This strange written conversation continued as they motored along.

That is not so bad to wait.

Wait? There are two of them out to get me - T and Y! They already destroyed my bees, chained me to a toilet and forced me to walk round with my bum on display.

I have had idea.
If you stay up
tonight late, see
T sleepwalking,
then you can tell

parents and she can take pill.
Sorting.

At least that is a good idea.

Pinja glanced in her mirror.

"Are you boys OK? You have much quiet. Anyway, we are arriving now."

"I'm fine," lied Soapy. As the car pulled into his drive his chest was pounding.

15
Yankenstein

Soapy lay in bed unable to sleep. He had managed to avoid seeing Topazz by saying that he didn't feel very well (which was partly true due to an unpleasant combination of mackerel squits and prank-fear reducing him to severe feebleness). He could tell that his mum was nervous with the two of them in the house together and she made a series of threats specifying just how dire the consequences would be for him if any more practical jokes happened that night. Soapy longed to tell her that the whole thing was the fault of cheese and eggs and shaggy superhuman beings but it was about as convincing as telling her that Scunthorpe had won the Champions League.

"Oh, and you haven't discovered anything missing in the house, have you?" said his mum.

"Er, what do you mean?"

"Well, I can scarcely believe it but your father left the back door open this morning when we went to visit your grandmother. Thieves could have just strolled in and helped themselves. Luckily, I think nothing came of it. Anyway, tell me if you notice anything missing."

"OK, I will Mum."

He thought back to the diary. On his return home he'd discovered that Topazz was downstairs looking at photos of London with her dad so he'd quickly skulked into her room and pushed the diary back into the inner zip pocket of the rucksack where Loogi had found it, praying that she hadn't noticed it was missing.

As he lay in bed that night, Soapy's mind returned to the problem of how to stop Yankenstein. The more he thought about it the more he realised that Arvo's plan was his best hope – to catch Topazz sleepwalking before she reached the eggs and then to tell or show one of the adults. They would surely then just give her the tablets to stop it and everything could return to normal. He had to do it. Reluctantly, he pulled himself out of bed and opened his door a fraction so he could see down the landing towards his cousin's bedroom door.

At just before midnight Soapy began to yawn heavily. He was cold but his eyelids were drooping. Should he go downstairs to make a coffee? No, it was too risky. He tried slapping his face a few times (which is surprisingly difficult to do) then continued to stand by the door peering through the crack towards the landing. The house was silent.

Ouch!

Soapy was aware of a sharp pain across his forehead. He was half-kneeling and had slipped down and cracked his temple on the brass door handle. He stood up woozily and felt for blood. Nothing. He looked at the clock: 2.13am.

I must have fallen asleep!

Soapy pulled his door a little further open and focused his crusty eyes on the landing.

Topazz's door was open.

Shaking himself awake, he padded down the dark corridor with a horrible feeling that Yankenstein might jump out on him at any moment. He approached the door and slowly peered inside the room. The bed was empty and there was no sign of Topazz. Could she be in the loo? The bathroom door was open but the light wasn't on.

Should he just wake his parents? What if she'd already turned into Yankenstein? Soapy hurried back to his room to look for a torch. As he was scrabbling around he thought he heard a sound outside in the gloom – a kind of rustling. He turned off his bedroom light and gently pulled back the curtain.

It was difficult to see anything at all outside but then came a familiar sound: a cat making a low warning screech. It was probably two of them fighting. But then, to Soapy's amazement, his garden was illuminated. The cat had wandered near to the garage security light and tripped the sensor causing the powerful light to flood the back of the house.

Soapy saw another movement and blinked. That was no cat – that was something much larger – a girl in pyjamas walking slowly through the grass. This was his big chance! Just as he was about to go and wake his parents, Topazz disappeared behind a large lilac bush. It was hard to see but it appeared that she was bending down. He could see movements but not make them out properly.

What was she doing?

Again, he turned to head for his parents' room but as he did so the security light went out and the garden was plunged into darkness. Soapy heard an unfamiliar sound outside and rushed back to the window. It sounded like a deep cackle. Although darkness shrouded the whole garden there was an unmistakable movement… not a cat, not a walking girl, but something large and hairy and chilling – something moving fast. It was too late!

Soapy heard the cackle again and realised that he had a chance to lock Yankenstein outside. He dashed onto the landing and hurled himself down the stairs and into the kitchen. The back door was wide open. He yanked it shut and locked it. He was safe.

His chest was heaving madly and he was out of breath. Soapy looked through the window at the blackness, wondering what Yankenstein was up to. A creak behind him made his heart stop. He turned round slowly.

It was his dad, rubbing his eyes.

"Soapy, what are you doing down here? It's after two o'clock."

"I, er, just needed a drink of water."

"Why were you looking out of the window?"

"I thought I saw something – it was just a cat."

"Listen, you'd better not be up to any of that prank nonsense again or we definitely will be sending you away to boarding school."

Soapy thought once more about canings, Latin and having his head flushed down grot-filled toilets.

"No, I promise I haven't done anything, Dad. I'm just going back to bed now."

He filled a glass of water and walked past his father whose brow still betrayed a hint of suspicion.

"Good night, Dad."

"Good night."

Back in his room, Soapy checked that his window was locked. There was no sign of movement outside. He shoved two heavy cupboards in front of the door and climbed into bed pulling his duvet tight.

Good night? Good? I've seen Yankenstein!

16
Transformation

Soapy sat in bed and shivered. It was now 3am.
There was no possibility of sleep and he didn't
want to drop off anyway. Yankenstein was on the
prowl. *Would it (she?) be stopped by a locked door?*
He thought back to some of the terrible pranks
that Prankenstein had carried out last year. There
was no way that a locked door or window would
stop such a creature. He was doomed. What on
earth could he do?

There was only one way to avoid a massive
pranking.

One escape.

One chance.

Soapy climbed out of bed and once more peeped
through the curtains. He could see nothing but
black, evil darkness. There was a monster out there.

He pulled back the line of science books on

his shelf and once more drew out the money box hidden there. It had some weight: there was something inside. Soapy hesitated. He was scared. If he opened the box there was no turning back. But how could such a small object hold such fear for him?

Soapy pressed the key into the lock and turned. He gripped the lid of the metal box and took a deep breath. Was he crazy?

Yes.

He wrenched open the lid and was nearly knocked over by the smell. Inside was the Manchego cheese that Arvo had found outside – the remains of the piece that Topazz had bought from Harrods, no doubt just to taunt him. Well now she was going to pay.

There was just one problem: Soapy didn't know if he would be able to eat even a tiny nibble of this foul-smelling stuff. He'd spent his whole life avoiding cheese until now – he wasn't even sure if he would be brave enough to pick it up.

Soapy stood in front of his long mirror wondering what it would be like to see himself transform into Prankenstein. If only it didn't involve cheese!

He reached into the box and lifted out a small lump of the dry, crusty Manchego. Immediately, he felt a tingling in his fingers that travelled up his arms and neck. He shivered and felt his throat become tickly. The hand holding the cheese began to shake and his fingers started to swell as if they were being inflated with gas.

I can't eat this! I'll die!

But then, in the distance, he heard a nerve-piercing howl: his mortal enemy.

Without hesitating, Soapy shoved the whole lump into his mouth and swallowed with not a single chew. His tongue and mouth felt like they would explode; it was like eating nuclear sherbet.

Soapy's now fat fingers dropped the money box and his whole body began to rock and shake as if he were experiencing his own personal earthquake. He belched, sneezed, coughed, hiccupped and farted with a shuddering volley of noise. His hands were now a sickly red and in the mirror, which itself was trembling with the vibration, he saw brown boils erupt all over his face giving it the appearance of a sickly turnip.

His feet now began to hiss, which was most disconcerting, and his whole body felt as if it were being pumped full of gravy. It was as if he were watching someone else; he was now wider, taller and meatier and his pyjamas stretched almost comically across a gorilla-like chest. Then, without warning, the shaking stopped and his bloated, now muscular body jolted then stopped quite still. Soapy's vision was suddenly razor sharp – he could see that he now had yellow eyes for a start.

He could also hear lots more than before and smell all sorts of things. He tried to move but couldn't; something told him that the transformation was not over. An abrupt gouging pain shot through his spine and he almost screamed. He contorted his face to counteract the ache which then began to subside. When he opened his eyes he had pointed ears and his whole body and face were coated with dark, wiry hairs.

And yet he didn't care. He felt strong and cunning and naughty and alive and ready to do something… but before the thought could complete itself, Soapy's mind went blank. After all, he was no longer Soapy.

17
Kids missing

Soapy's dad woke up early hoping to get a round of golf with Finn before the course filled up. He was only half awake as he trudged down the stairs towards the coffee machine in the kitchen. The first thing he noticed was that the kitchen looked strangely empty. Well, very empty actually. After that he saw that the worktops were all hidden under great stacks of packets and tins.

He turned around and scanned the room. Every surface was completely covered with cans, boxes, jars, packaging, plastic bags, wrappers, tubs and pots and they were all empty.

Thieves? No one was that hungry. He checked the fridge and the cupboards just to be sure – they were completely bare. What was going on?

And then he realised the other reason why the kitchen looked so strange and empty. The big breakfast table and eight wooden chairs were missing. His brain was now alert and trying to make sense of everything and it rapidly came to a dismal conclusion. Pranks...

Soapy's dad called up the stairs for his wife to come quickly while he considered whether to call 999. Was this an emergency? *Someone has eaten all of our crackers, officer.* Then he realised that he hadn't even checked the rest of the house.

With dread he hurried through to the living room. That was empty too, except that the carpet was covered in a fourteen centimetre layer of Rice Krispies. *Where was the furniture? The TV? The vases of flowers?*

Soapy's mum came tumbling down the stairs wrapping a robe around herself. Her face was like a cartoon drawing of fear.

"Not again? Not again!"

Her husband didn't know what to say.

He scurried around the house checking the other rooms, hearing his wife's groans and shrieks as he went. All of the furniture was missing. He reached for the keys to unlock the back door and heard someone else coming down the stairs. It was Ivette, holding out her hands and looking queasy.

"Why is the bath filled with food? It's all mixed together in this disgusting gloop."

Soapy's mum and dad didn't answer her. Instead they pushed open the back door and stepped into the garden. The first thing that they noticed was the noise – the sound of vehicles and sirens and people shouting and raving. Along the road there were police cars and fire engines and most of the residents of the street, ranting away in a great cacophony.

Then they saw their furniture. It was dangling. The leather sofa, the chairs, the kitchen table, the footrests, the cupboards, the lamps, the vases and even the TV were all hanging on strings from the branches of their big sycamore tree, like dreary outsized Christmas decorations. Mrs Thompson was speechless for a moment then her mouth exploded with so many words that none of her utterances made sense.

"WhattheheavensisgoingonIdonotbelievethis
someonehasgonetoofarthisisanoutrageascandal
andIamgoingtofindoutwhodiditandIamgoingto
havethemputinjailforaveryverylongtime!"

Mr Thompson was a lot quieter. He was looking
back at the house and simply said, "You might not
want to turn round, dear."

Of course she did, and what she saw was her
large expensive detached executive house completely
smeared in chocolate and covered with millions
of hundreds and thousands.

They stood and gawped.

"Looks like the world's biggest and ugliest cake,"
wailed Soapy's dad.

But his wife didn't hear. She had wandered
around to the front of the house where she was
looking at her husband's brand new car. It was
wrapped in spotty gift paper and tied with a giant
pink bow. She decided not to tell him.

Ivette came and saw the house and furniture
and started laughing. She simply couldn't help
herself. Amid the cries of their neighbours
complaining to the police about disgraceful pranks,
Soapy's mum rushed past Ivette and back indoors
where she saw Dove and Finn staring at the

ruination of the house.

"What is going on? And have you seen Topazz?" said Dove. "She's not in her room."

Soapy's mum didn't know what to say. Instead she scampered up the stairs and pushed open Soapy's bedroom door.

"Pugh? Pugh!"

He was gone. She dashed into the bathroom and saw the stupendous tub-soup of beans, pasta, yogurt, mince, eggs, raisins, rice, milk, curry powder, treacle, bananas, bread, sardines and thirty other foods all stirred together in a glutinous grey stew. But there were no children. All four parents rushed round the house and garden calling out the names of the cousins to no avail.

Finn tried to get hold of a policeman standing by his patrol car out on the road but the officer was

surrounded by a ring of enraged householders
wanting their homes de-mangled and demanding
that the culprits be discovered pronto.

"I'll call 999," said Mrs Thompson after getting
no response from Soapy's mobile, only to discover
it was engaged.

Dove's face was pale. "Perhaps they've gone off
together – you know, for a bit of fun... But where
can they be? Topazz isn't answering her phone."

"I have an idea," said Soapy's dad. He called
Arvo and Loogi's house on his mobile.

"Hello... Arvo? It's Soapy's father here. You
haven't seen him this morning, have you? Or his
American cousin? No? Oh, it's just that they're
missing.... Yes... no... we don't know.... the noise?
Oh, the pranks have started again; our house is
covered with hundreds and thousands. Of what?
No, they're cake decorations – little sugar things.
Yes, like Hansel and Gretel... OK, thanks, bye."

The others looked at him with little hope in
their eyes. He shook his head. "I say we go and
start looking ourselves."

A few miles across town, the morning had started
serenely and prank-free. There were no people

shouting in the street and no police cars or fire engines dealing with garden swing seats taped to the tops of lamp posts or satellite dishes full of onions.

Arvo had put down the phone after the call from Mr Thompson and gone straight to Loogi. They spoke quietly to each other.

"Soapy he is missing, also Topazz," said Arvo.

Loogi registered little surprise. "As I was fearing. She got to the eggs I am suspecting…"

"And turned into Yankenstein before Soapy could tell parents?"

"Most of the likely, yes." Loogi put down the crossword book he was holding.

"And Soapy?"

"Yankenstein may have done taking him somewhere. Or I fear other outcome…"

Arvo knew what his brother was thinking. "That Soapy feared Yankenstein's prank power and so he turned to Prankenstein to be saving himself?"

Loogi nodded. "That is what I am concluding. They are having Prank War."

The boys decided there and then that they must help their beleaguered friend. They snuck down to the kitchen of their house and picked up

drinks, biscuits, nuts and other supplies. They put them in backpacks, picked up their mobiles and all the money they had, then wrote a brief note to their parents.

Don't worry, we are looking for Soapy. Will be back soon. A & L.

As quietly as prowling cats, they stole out of the door, climbed on their bikes and headed in the direction of their friend's now sugar-coated house.

Half an hour later another series of phone calls was exchanged between the Twince's parents and the Thompsons who were anxious to know if Soapy had turned up at Arvo and Loogi's. Pinja made the final call once she'd found her sons' note.

"I am having the further bad news – there are now four children missing."

18
Pranktown

It didn't take long for word about the mass pranking to spread via social media. By mid-morning local radio reporters were roving about the streets around Soapy's house interviewing confused residents whose garden ponds now contained electric eels or whose mobility scooters had been yarn-bombed. Soon after this, national newspaper journalists descended on the town followed by TV crews from the BBC, ITN and four American networks.

"I'm standing here in a once quiet, leafy suburb," said one TV news correspondent to a hurriedly assembled camera crew. "As you can probably hear, this place is no longer quiet – its streets are full of outraged, bewildered residents demanding that the police do something urgent. Welcome to Pranktown, as it's now being called."

The reporters rushed round, microphones in hand, gathering stories of as many incidents as they could, trying to find the most scandalous one. One of them pounded up to Soapy's dad as he tried to catch the attention of the policeman who was still buried inside a mob of ranting householders.

"Excuse me, sir, Mr er…" said the reporter.

"Thompson," said Soapy's father without even thinking.

"Have you been pranked too, sir? What kind of awful things have happened to you, your property or your loved ones? Anything horrid or grisly, maybe?"

Soapy's dad looked down at the woman's notebook and saw a scribbled list:

- Hairdresser: car filled with sausages
- Bypass: traffic cones replaced with Barbies
- Leisure centre: swimming pool filled with jelly (pineapple)
- Golf course: all greens painted orange

"Yes, our house has been pranked like everyone else's," growled Mr Thompson, "but that isn't our biggest problem right now."

The reporter's eyebrows lifted a notch. "Oh, and what has happened to you, sir, may I ask?"

At this point, Soapy's mum bustled across and interrupted her husband.

"Listen, we'll give you the story if you help us by putting the word out across TV, radio, the web and other media channels, OK?"

The reporter almost fell backwards with the force of Mrs Thompson's glare.

"Er, yes, of course – that's what we do – spread news. How can we help?"

Soapy's mum pulled the reporter away from the noise and bustle. "My son and niece are missing. They disappeared last night."

An hour later, Arvo and Loogi watched the scene from a small hill just two hundred metres from Soapy's house. They saw flashing blue lights, traffic jams, BBC radio cars with giant aerials and people milling about everywhere, many yelling and pointing.

Arvo exhaled. "Well, there is not the need to be going nearer – Prankenstein and Yankenstein have been the busy-busy brutes in the night."

"It is too much of the risk anyway," said Loogi.

"We might be observed and suffer the capture. We must be staying out of the sight."

"Correct, but how are we going to find the location of Soapy?"

Loogi pulled out his phone and switched it on. He tried calling Soapy but there was no answer. "I will look to news on Auntie Beeb," he said opening a web browser. The BBC local news headline was:

PRANK EXPLOSION A MYSTERY

The Twince clicked a video report and waited for it to load. The film eventually came to life and the brothers watched in disbelief as they saw a trail of pranking mayhem far beyond anything that Prankenstein had carried out the previous year. They listened carefully to the news.

"The practical jokes have been reported in three separate areas of town. First, on the exclusive Elm Trees estate around a road of large detached houses called The Cloisters. Then there are reports of similar shocking pranks in the north of the town around the pooter factory and another cluster has been

**reported in the south of the town near to
Minty Badger College..."**

"This is being of most interest," said Arvo,
squinting at the small screen. "It is suggesting that
one beastie has gone north and one to the south."

Loogi nodded. "Truth. Let us read more."
He clicked on some more news links and found
a statement from the town's Chief Constable.

"Investigations are ongoing and I have all of my
best officers out there determined to apprehend
the culprits. We are still gathering leads but at
present we believe we are dealing with either
a gang of malicious circus clowns, a group of
deranged chefs or possibly a seven-foot toddler.
Members of the public are advised not to
approach any of these suspects."

"Otch, these coppers are of the useless variety,"
said Arvo. "We are only eleven years but have far
superior detective skills. We are knowing exactly
the truth, not this poopycock."

"I am thinking it is poppycock," said Loogi.

"Precise," said Arvo. "At least they are not

mentioning the missing children."

Loogi scrolled down the page. "Oh," he muttered. "Look at this."

> **BREAKING NEWS: Four local children missing**
>
> Newspaper sources are reporting that four local children have been reported missing this morning. Details are currently sketchy but two are said to be cousins, Pugh and Topazz Thompson, and two are believed to be Latvian brothers called Argos and Looni. Further details to follow.

Arvo stamped his foot. "This is outrage of disgrace and non-justice. LATVIAN!"

"Hey, it is not so much bad for you – people now are thinking I am nutcase." Loogi tried some local newspaper websites to see if there was more information. Everywhere were tales of shocking pranks along with brief stories describing the missing children.

"'The Chronical' says we are five year-old Lithuanians called Arso and Luigi," said Loogi.

"That is why they are chronic. What does Gazza say?"

"Fool brother. Gazza is dippy-daft genius

Geordie footballer of 1990s. You mean 'Gazette'."

"Whatevers."

"'Gazette' says identical sisters Nervo and Loopy are reported missing. 'The Mighty Metro' says we are called Aero and Boogi."

"Oh dear," said Arvo, changing his tone.

"What, you have the disgust they are calling us girls?"

"No. The report also has the add that the police are out searching for us now with sniffy dogs and poking sticks."

Loogi switched off his phone. "Otch, they can also be tracing our position from phone signal – we have acted like the div."

Arvo climbed on his bike. "Correct. We must do the scarper instant. You go north and I south – there is more chance to find our friend then."

Loogi nodded saying that they would be less likely to be found if they split up too. They agreed to put their phones back on briefly at eleven o'clock and to contact each other for an update. Arvo wished his twin brother good luck then sped off on his slightly bent BMX bike. He was back eight seconds later.

"Which way is being south?"

19
On the trail

Loogi made his way north across the town with
some difficulty. His bike was heavy and slow,
probably something to do with the fact that it had
once been part of one of his father's fusion sculptures.
Olof had attempted to make a pedal-powered
mobile aquarium but had given up when the water
sloshed about everywhere and sea-life escaped
each time he went round a corner. The bad news
for Loogi was that the bike still had a large plastic
tank welded to the back. And it smelt of fish.

After riding for twenty minutes he spotted the
first clue that one of the morphed pranksters had
been in the vicinity. There was a small row of
shops along the road and a crowd of people had
gathered outside them and were pointing. There
were also people on ladders adjusting something

above the windows on some of them. It soon
became apparent what had happened when Loogi
read the shop signs.

"Prankenstein or Yankenstein for sure," said
Loogi to himself, cycling past among sniggers
from some of the onlookers. He then came to the
town's small industrial estate and here too was
evidence of pranking. The workers at Pinkerton's
Pasta were all standing in the factory car park
looking up at the small wind turbine belonging
to Eco-Chic Solutions next door. Loogi stared
up at the juddering rotor of the turbine and saw
that the blades were trailing great streamers of
flopping spaghetti. The whole thing made an eerie
whooshing noise and squawking rooks, starlings

and pigeons flapped
around it trying
to grab beakfuls
for lunch.

Loogi took a photo
of the mayhem then
carried on pedalling until
he reached a large housing
estate. On the corner was a café which made
Loogi realise that he was thirsty. He parked
his peculiar bike round the back and wandered
inside. The man behind the counter was talking
to a woman holding a baby.

"I'm really sorry, Shanna, but there's only ham,
chicken or tuna. All of our cheese disappeared last
night in that break-in and I just can't afford to buy
any more. I can do you a salad."

Loogi bought a bottle of rhubarb juice then
slipped outside and looked at his watch. It was
almost eleven o'clock. He switched on his phone
and called his brother who answered immediately.

"You have not been suffering the discovery by
authorities, then?" said Arvo. "I have been noticing
many of the police but they have not seen me yet."

"News good," said Loogi. "I have been making

discovery myself, of much interest. Pranking on industrial scale is here in the north of town and I am thinking it is Prankenstein doing this."

"How so?"

"A café here has experienced strange cheese loss in the night."

"Ah, I too have been seeing prank evidences in the south and the clues that maybe Yankenstein has been here on prowl."

Loogi looked around to check no one was watching him. "What clues?"

"A supermarket of the mini-variety had sign on door saying: 'sorry no eggs' – I am thinking that maybe Yankenstein has done the thefting of them so it can stay in the beastie condition."

"Hmmm, that is making some of the sense… what pranking indications have you been observing?"

Arvo let out a light chortle. "Ah, much creative jest. I first headed for the college as it was being mentioned on that news report. It is large and simple to locate. It has giant letters on side of building spelling 'MINTY BADGER COLLEGE' except now they are saying 'TRY BAD MING COLLEGE'."

"That brings some amuse but prankster has not used first E – Yankenstein would be feeble crossword compiler."

"Fool brother, that is not mattering. We have made discovery that Prankenstein is in north and Yankenstein in south but we must formulate plan to rescue Soapy."

Loogi frowned. "You say fool but I already am making such plan. I detect that the two creature cousins are arming themselves ahead of big battle. They require cheese and eggs to stay naughty and they are clearly being greedy for them."

"So what is plan?"

"We head to high ground – to hill. We first make purchase of ponky cheese. We do much wafting of this. Maybe smells will be attracting Prankenstein."

Arvo, who was hiding in some bushes in the college grounds, tried to keep his voice low. "That might be working but what do we do if Prankenstein arrives? He is crazy monster with muscles of bulge – he could grab us and do much of the pulverising."

"Correct. First we must also be purchasing large net."

20
The chase is on

When Arvo finished talking to his brother he checked his phone for further news stories about pranks. Amongst the reports about the four missing children there was an update on the local BBC page saying that a spate of pranks had been reported on farms to the east of the town. He looked on his map app and found a small patch of woodland next to a quiet country road to the east of the town and texted

Loogi to meet him there once he had bought a net.

Arvo jumped on his bike and headed for a convenience store across the road from the college so that he could buy some cheese to try and lure Prankenstein. As he dismounted next to the shop, a white BMW screeched to a halt on the pavement outside. It was a police car.

For a moment Arvo froze, then doors opened on both sides of the car and a uniformed policeman stepped out along with his mother.

"Arvo!" screeched Pinja, rushing towards him. "Thank the heavens you are being safe. We tracked down your phone signal." She crossed the pavement and reached out her arms towards him. He was about to speak and hug her when some peculiar urge made him stop then jump back on his bike and start pedalling madly up the pavement through a crowd of people.

"Oi!" growled the policeman who started giving chase.

"Hey, you rascally berk!" squawked Pinja. "You cannot be abandoning your mother – I only just am finding you!"

But he was gone. Arvo tried to call out, "Sorry, Mother I will do much explaining later," but the sound was drowned out by traffic and people shouting.

The policeman caught up initially and made a lunge to grab him but only succeeded in landing on an elderly lady's shopping trolley. She whacked the officer on the back with her umbrella and shouted, "Help, police!"

The officer rolled over, grabbed the bruising brolly and said, "I am the police, madam."

"Then arrest yerself," said the old lady.

Arvo pedalled frantically down a narrow side street and along a riverside cycle path where cars couldn't follow him. After two more frantic minutes he stopped and pulled out his phone, speed dialling Loogi.

"Get rid of your mobile, Loogi! The police can trace it."

"OK," came the faint reply before the line went dead.

Arvo then looked around. The police would be on him again at any moment. He considered throwing his phone in the river when a figure came bobbing along the path: a jogger. Arvo waited for him to pass then cycled up behind him and very deftly placed his mobile in the jogger's tracksuit hood.

"That'll confuse them," he whispered before cycling off towards the east.

Loogi was cycling on the outskirts of town shortly after Arvo's call. He was wondering what to do with his mobile when a beating sound overhead started to get louder. A helicopter. He looked up. The chopper slowed down then hovered just above him. He turned left and the helicopter followed. In the distance he could hear a police siren. Loogi wasted no time. He hurled his phone over a garden fence and began to pedal like mad. The phone landed on a barbecue and melted instantly.

Loogi had no idea where he was but noticed a sign saying 'Middleton Country Park'. He turned off the road, through a gate and headed down a bumpy lane with the police helicopter tracking his moves. To the right, Loogi noticed a large cluster of trees. Without hesitating he turned onto the grass and cycled into the wood, his heavy bike crashing through fallen branches and knotty brambles. He turned left and headed into a dense part of the small forest, noticing that the helicopter was no longer above him. A car certainly couldn't come this way. Had he escaped?

21
Kidnapped?

As his twin brother Loogi disappeared deeper into the woods, Arvo was still in town, trying to evade capture and wondering how he would be able to make his way out into the countryside without being spotted. It was looking increasingly unlikely that the Twince would be able to rescue their friend Soapy.

What would happen if Prankenstein and Yankenstein were truly at war? It would be pandemonium, havoc, catastrophe – that amount of pranking could destroy the planet!

Arvo had a more pressing problem: he was also no longer sure which way was east. It was now around midday and the sun should be in the south, he told himself. The trouble was that it was a cloudy day and he couldn't see much of the sky between the buildings.

I need to get up a bit higher.

He saw a multi-storey car park two roads away but it would be too risky to ride there as the police probably now had been issued with his description. He hid his bike behind some boxes at the back of an Italian restaurant, took off his jumper and put it in his backpack. Next he put on his cap; at least he now looked slightly different.

His heart beating, convinced that lots of people were watching him, Arvo crossed the busy streets and headed for the car park. He climbed the concrete stairs, which smelled of wee, then finally arrived at the top of the building. No one had even glanced at him.

From here he saw the milky sun behind a cloud and from there worked out which way was east. He looked in that direction and wondered how Loogi was doing.

How was Soapy doing? And Topazz?

In the distance he could see the hazy countryside. There was also a white helicopter buzzing there. The police? It could well be. Anyway, that's the direction he had to go.

As Arvo ran back down to find his bike he lost his bearings and ended up on a crowded street of shops. In one of them that sold TVs there was a giant window banked full of huge screens all showing the face of a newsreader. And then another face appeared. His! He was there, on telly, along with his brother – two awful photos taken last year in school. He rushed inside the shop so he could hear and stood in front of the one TV that had some sound, and listened to the newsreader.

"...as well as the missing Estonian brothers, police are continuing their search for local schoolboy Pugh Thompson and his cousin Topazz Thompson."

Another photo appeared: Topazz's teeth filled the screen and made him wince. The reporter continued.

"We are now going to hear a live statement from Chief Constable Archibald Lavery."

A huge, red-faced man filled the screen, looking very serious. He read from a piece of paper.

"After extensive investigations this morning, we are now convinced that there is a link

between the outbreak of pranks carried out across the town last night and the disappearance of these children. The Etonian lads have been spotted by officers and are still at large although believed to be safe. Pug and Toepad, however, have not been seen since last night and there is now a serious concern that they may have been kidnapped by the two mysterious creatures recently seen heading towards the village of Devere to the east of the town. We are deploying extra forces there along with a special operations unit and police dogs plus any other animals we consider will come in handy. I am now going to show an appeal to the kidnappers by one of the children's mothers."

Arvo stood and gaped, his mind racing.

Special operations? Does that mean guns? And how do I get to Devere? And why are we at large? I'm quite small for my age.

His thoughts were interrupted by the face of a woman who Arvo didn't recognise. She was tanned and blonde with two black streaks down

her face where her make-up had mingled with tears. She was sobbing and barely able to speak.

"My name is, is Dove Thompson, and I am the mommy of a beautiful girl called Topazz who you monsters out there have kidnapped. She is a sweet, innocent girl – and one of the best surfers for her age – and I want her back. I am appealing to you kidnappers to return her right away. Oh, and her cousin too – Soapy, I mean Pugh. Please, please let them go. And if you don't my very large angry husband will find you and smash your face in."

Arvo had seen enough. Pulling down his cap he shuffled out of the shop and made his way back to his bike. He looked at it and thought, *No, the police are looking for a kid on a bike. I will run to Devere. Or maybe walk.*

By this time, Loogi too had abandoned his bike. It was simply much too difficult to ride through the woods. The helicopter had at least moved away much to his relief, but now he was lost and thirsty again. After wandering through the trees

for a little longer, still heading vaguely east, Loogi came to the edge of the forest where open country stretched out. There was a farm to the right. He decided to risk knocking on the door and asking for a drink.

A small elderly woman answered.

"Er, hello lady, I am being lost and I am getting thirsty and, er…"

"Oh come in, come in," said the woman, pulling back the door. "Not safe for you to be out on your own with all these wild creatures on the loose. Is lemonade all right for you? I made it myself. About four years ago."

Loogi nodded and cautiously sat down in the long, dark kitchen.

The small woman passed him a cloudy glass. "You've not seen any of those missing children, have you? Awful business. They reckon those yeti-things have got two of them. The others are

Russian or something – probably spies anyway."

"Estonian actual," said Loogi, wishing he hadn't.

She ignored him. "Piece of cabbage cake? This is my son Gunter's favourite."

"Erm no thank you." Loogi's eyes flickered around wondering if there was anyone else in the house.

"I've heard on the radio that the police have followed them towards Devere now – that's only a mile up the track here. On the news they said that two of the squad cars had been vandalised; one had been given monster truck wheels – whatever they are – and the other sprayed pink and the roof cut off."

"Which direction is this Devere, please?"

The woman pointed. "Up there, you know, just next to the safari park."

She turned back...but Loogi had already gone.

22
Closing in

Anyone driving west along the B7406 that day would have been witness to something you don't see very often. A Mr Icy-Nicey ice cream van was being driven at 89mph along the middle of the road with music blaring from its wobbly rooftop speaker, 'Bat out of Hell' to be precise. The driver was a hairy, squat figure with yellow eyes and pointed ears, cackling madly and squirting raspberry juice through the window at passers-by. In pursuit of the van was a white Ford Focus with giant wheels, flashing blue lights and a siren, followed by a peculiar pink convertible police car.

Just as the supercharged lolly-seller looked like it was about to collide with a lorry carrying zombie costumes, Prankenstein pulled the steering wheel violently to the left and careered down a bumpy track marked 'Sunnyvale Farm'.

Meanwhile, nearby at Devere Safari Park,

a crime squad helicopter was chasing a second manic hairy figure across a field. The creature was riding a fluorescent green giraffe.

"Pursuing Suspect Two across tiger enclosure," reported the pilot over his radio. "Creature is travelling in direction of Sunnyvale Farm. Over."

A bewildered police officer – in the pink car – shouted a reply into his handset. "Message received Skywatch. We are still in pursuit of Suspect One in the ice-cream van, also heading towards Sunnyvale Farm. Can you confirm if Suspect Two has kidnapped child?"

"Negative."

"This one appears to be alone in the ice cream van too. Will report to HQ that we have no sighting of missing Thompson children. Over."

Just a few hundred yards away, on the top of a small hill and hidden by gorse bushes, Loogi watched a great cloud of dust rise up as the rock anthem-powered van blasted along the farm track towards a long low house surrounded by large agricultural buildings and beyond that dense woodland. The two bizarre squad cars slowed down as the ice-cream van screeched to a halt and Prankenstein scuttled out, disappearing

with panther-like speed into a big grey barn.

Meanwhile, Arvo had finally escaped the town by sticking to back roads and footpaths until he was out into open country. He headed east, looking for hills or woodland, hoping to find his twin brother before the police found him. He hadn't managed to buy a net and he had no idea how he was going to rescue Soapy but he was determined not to let his friend down.

After Arvo had been walking across fields for some time he heard the unmistakable sound of a rotor chopping through the air rhythmically above and approaching fast. He looked up, saw the helicopter, then ran towards a fat, twisted oak tree in a nearby hedge. He began to climb its lumpy branches until he was well hidden. Arvo peered down from his high position and saw that there was a narrow road on the other side of the hedge. At that moment a piercing sound caused him to whip his head around.

"Arrrrrrrgggggghhhhhhyyyyeeeeeehhhhaaaa!"

He clung hard to the trunk and tried to stay hidden as four spindly vibrant green legs charged past. He crouched and saw a lime-coloured giraffe galumphing along, its eyes wide with panic, and a hairy, hooting, jiggling creature surfing on its back, munching a box of eggs and waving the Stars and Stripes flag.

Yankenstein!

Arvo almost fell out of the tree but another noise caught his attention. He watched boggle-eyed as a large silver car shot past along the lane, its windows open and the heads of Mrs Thompson and a huge tanned man hanging out and shouting instructions to the driver who appeared to be Soapy's dad. As the car disappeared Arvo looked back and saw the giraffe vault a hedge and gallop towards some grey buildings in the near distance.

He was considering climbing down from the tree and following when he heard a squeal of tyres and a familiar orange VW camper van came pooping and rattling down the lane, a great plume of dark fumes rising up behind it. His mother held the wheel with his father raging in the passenger's seat and holding what appeared to be a huge woodcarver's mallet.

The camper van spluttered away but not far behind came a whole convoy of TV and radio crews along with hungry-looking newspaper journalists.

The vehicles roared towards the farm, leaving a moment's blissful silence before a new rumpus, this time non-mechanical, caused Arvo to peer down from his leafy hideout.

A short, sweating, red-faced man came lurching along the lane, his feet heavy on the tarmac, his mouth panting for air and his fingers bent and twitching. Arvo could just about read the logo on the muddy white apron that he was wearing:

Mr Icy-Nicey

"I will not give up," he gasped. "I keep going, I reach you, I get you and then I will scrunch up your face."

Just half a mile ahead, at that moment, a blonde bushy figure somersaulted down from the exhausted animal it was riding, gave a derisive whoop and then slid open a metal door at the back of a large grey barn.

23
Trapped

Loogi crouched low and sidled along behind hedges making his way back towards the farm where everyone was heading.

When he got closer, he could see people and vehicles everywhere. There were at least twenty police officers, some with guns, plus dog handlers and people putting up barriers and hatched yellow tape. Overhead, two helicopters buzzed and someone with a twanging tannoy was ordering the press and TV crews to stand back.

"THIS IS A DANGEROUS EMERGENCY SITUATION!" boomed the voice. "KEEP BACK BEHIND THE TAPE OR RISK ARREST."

Loogi felt uncomfortable where he could easily be discovered. He looked around for cover and saw an old rusty tractor with filthy windows further along the field. Moving slowly he edged along the hedge just a couple of metres from two bulky policemen on the other side. Reaching the tractor, Loogi crept around the back and tried a door. The handle, though stiff, gently clunked down and the door opened. Inside he was surprised at how high up the seat was. The mud-spattered windscreen would certainly hide him from view but he couldn't see what was going on outside.

Taking a risk, Loogi opened the door of the tractor again, slipped down, pulled out his crusty hanky and quietly spat on it. He checked to see if anyone was looking his way. Fortunately, the whole crowd of adults was focused on the big grey barn in the other direction. Taking a considerable risk, Loogi clambered onto the front wheel, reached up and as rapidly as he could, scrubbed the windscreen so that a small clear circle of glass was created. He then hopped down and crept back into the cab.

Through his spyhole, Loogi now had a good view of the whole farmyard. The sight was shocking. Armed police officers stood around the large grey steel and concrete barn, some with savage Alsatians pulling at their leashes. Further back behind the tape were clusters of TV crews filming news

bulletins along with journalists busily scribbling.

And what of Prankenstein and Yankenstein?

His silent question was abruptly answered by the man with the braying tannoy.

"THIS IS THE POLICE. YOU ARE SURROUNDED BY ARMED OFFICERS. REPEAT, YOU ARE NOW TRAPPED INSIDE THE BUILDING AND HAVE NO HOPE OF ESCAPE. THIS MESSAGE IS ADDRESSED TO BOTH, CRE-, ER FUGITIVES. COME OUT AND GIVE YOURSELVES UP."

Loogi gulped. Poor old Soapy – what could be done for him now? Loogi felt powerless. His only consolation was that at least he had a great view of the action. It was highly unlikely that anyone would discover him now.

At that moment, the door of the tractor creaked open and Loogi's heart nearly erupted. He was about to scream when Arvo's face appeared with a smile.

"Hello, brother."

"You double berk! I am nearly doing the big poo of my pants you scared me so much," whispered Loogi.

Arvo held out his hands. "What could I do? Be knocking on the door? There are more cops here than at royal wedding!"

"SShhhh!"

"I am seeing you climb in tractor. I was in tree back there. Am I right in fearing Prankenstein and Yankenstein are both being trapped in this farm building?"

Loogi nodded. "Correct. It is not looking so goodly for Soapy. Either he is getting the big prank-maul by his enemy in barn, or he will be arrested on national TV."

"You forgot mashed by dog. Or shot."

"We are needing highly superior plan."

"Or miracle."

The brothers peered through the tiny peephole and saw the sliding door of the barn still shut, with the ring of uniformed enforcers standing and waiting.

Behind the police tape a BBC film crew

bustled a large, dirty man in front of the cameras. His face was crimson and heavily lined. Next to him a tiny old lady grinned and occasionally prodded people with her umbrella.

"We are broadcasting live from Sunnyvale Farm," said the reporter, trying to look serious, "in the middle of one of the most remarkable fugitive chases in British police history. We believe that two mysterious, dangerous assailants responsible for hundreds of shocking pranks are trapped inside this building which is now surrounded by armed special forces. I have here Gunter Drench, owner of the farm and his mother, Prudence. Mr Drench, I gather you witnessed one of the suspects enter your barn?"

"Too right. An 'orrible 'airy job he was too. Not 'uman – more like an alien in a monkey suit. Reminded me of my Uncle Des."

"And did you see this, er, figure, Mrs Drench?" asked the reporter, thrusting a microphone at the old lady next to him.

"There were two of 'em and I saw 'em both. I threw a mangelwurzel at the first one – cheeky scoundrel, hiding in our barn."

"Can you describe the creatures for our viewers?"

"Well, they was like somethin' off Doctor Who. Woolly, smelly, nasty, rude and as strong as an ox. Bit like Gunter here."

The reporter turned back to the camera. "So, there we are. Is this Britain's answer to Bigfoot or perhaps the famed Beast of Bodmin on holiday? Have we discovered extra-terrestrial life or is it just a fancy dress party that went horribly wrong? The police have issued an ultimatum to these shadowy outlaws. Now the waiting game begins..."

24
The government steps in

Arvo and Loogi were discussing whether they should create a diversion by jumping out of the tractor, making a lot of noise and then running away across the field.

"This might be distracting police sufficient for Soapy-Prankenstein to make the barn escape," said Arvo.

"And it might be sufficient for us to have the mangling by savage hounds."

"That I would not be enjoying much."

"Anyways," said Loogi, "creating diversion is something only happens in Beano or foolish film – when was the last time you did creating diversion?"

"OK, OK, Alecy-smart brother, what is your plan?"

Loogi pulled a lump of plastic-wrapped

mozzarella from his backpack. "I am not knowing but it may involve cheese."

Just forty-seven metres away from the two boys, the BBC TV crew turned their attention to six haggard adults standing in a grumpy huddle.

The reporter addressed the camera once again.

"I have here the parents of Pugh Thompson, the missing local schoolboy, along with the parents of his American cousin Topazz. Next to them are the parents of the Estonian twins who are also missing but who have been spotted recently in the nearby town. Mrs Thompson, is there any news on your son?"

A bead of sweat trickled down the nose of Soapy's mum as she turned to the camera.

"Yes, the news is that we are very cross – very VERY cross. Half of the county constabulary is here to chase these – these nincompoop ape things trapped in this barn. Why aren't they finding my son? They should be scouring the countryside, not standing here like uniformed muppets."

"Er, strong opinions there from one of the parents," stuttered the reporter. He turned to Topazz's father. "Your daughter is also missing.

How do you feel and why have you come here to this farm?"

Finn's eyes were boiling. "How do you think I feel – what kind of dumbo question is that?"

Dove butted in. "Listen you media buffoons. We want our daughter back – we came here because your genius British police told us they thought these two furry goons had kidnapped her. Now we have come all the way out here and everyone tells us there are no kids here at all."

The reporter was about to speak when Pinja and Olof pushed in front of the camera. "Hey, what about my boys?" said a big-eyed Pinja. "Estonians need to have the finding too. I want cops without guns and maybe with sniffers."

Olof stepped forward lifting the stout carving mallet above his shoulder, growling, "If two beasts in barn have done the lunching of

my twince, I make them into mushy pulp."

Seventeen seconds after the interview, all three hundred people around the farm turned their heads to see two police motorcycles draw up to the barriers followed by a large black car with darkened windows. It stopped and three burly security men jumped out talking into their sleeves. A moment later a thin, smartly dressed woman got out and stood up. Everyone could tell that she was very important. All cameras immediately pointed in her direction and a senior police officer hurried over to speak to her.

The Twince watched the scene unfold from their musty tractor cab, the cheese now warm in Loogi's hands, his brain still fizzing with ideas.

For two minutes a hushed conversation continued before the senior police officer spoke into his radio. The smart woman was then ushered to the other side of the barriers well away from the press, and surrounded by armed figures.

Mrs Thompson whispered to her husband, "That looks like the Home Secretary – what on earth is she doing here?" His answer was drowned out by the tannoy.

"THIS IS AN IMPORTANT ANNOUNCEMENT. THE GOVERNMENT HAS NOW DECLARED THAT THIS HAS BECOME A MILITARY OPERATION. REPEAT. THIS IS NOW A MILITARY OPERATION AND FOR YOUR OWN SAFETY ALL CIVILIANS, INCLUDING THE PRESS, ARE REQUIRED TO WITHDRAW TO THE MAIN ROAD WITHIN THE NEXT TEN MINUTES. ANYONE REFUSING TO COMPLY WILL BE ARRESTED."

A great babble of noise surged up from the media teams at this point and a line of policemen immediately began to usher them and the Thompsons and the Twince's parents towards their cars and vans.

Arvo and Loogi were not watching that, however; their heads were turned to the side and their eyes were tracking something that the reporters could not see. Approaching the farm from a lane on the other side of the buildings was a convoy of six roaring army tanks.

25
Take aim

Arvo put his head in his hands. "This is getting the worse."

The six huge tanks were spread in a semi-circle, their great jutting guns pointing towards the barn where Prankenstein and Yankenstein were imprisoned. Further vehicles had joined them, together with missile launchers and camouflaged soldiers with laser-guided weapons.

"We must be doing something," croaked Loogi. "Or Soapy may be nuked live on TV."

Arvo sighed. "What can we do? Even if we are telling truth they will not believe us. Anyway, we are being the only non-military people here now – if we do climbing out of this cab they will probably bazooka us."

Once more, the air shuddered with the booming sound of the tannoy.

"THIS MESSAGE IS FOR THE TWO FUGITIVES IN THE BARN. THIS IS YOUR FINAL WARNING. YOU HAVE THIRTY MINUTES TO COME OUT AND GIVE YOURSELVES UP BEFORE WE MOVE IN WITH FIREPOWER. REPEAT, THIRTY MINUTES."

The Twince agreed that it would probably be best if they didn't get hit by an army rocket, so, trembling quietly, they pushed down the handle of the tractor cab door, inched it open and dropped down onto the grass just a few metres away from a line of soldiers with heavy-duty machine guns and grenade launchers. Staying behind the hedge they edged along away from the farm.

A mile away Dove Thompson tried calling Topazz's mobile once more. She had already left nineteen messages but she knew that it was useless. Just as she switched off her phone, a reporter scurried over and thrust a voice recorder in her face.

"Mrs Thompson, the TV microphones have

just picked up a tannoy message from the farm. The military are going to open fire on the barn in twenty-eight minutes. Do you want to respond to that?"

"Yes." She rolled up a sleeve and punched him on the leg. He grunted an 'oof' and fell backwards causing eleven other journalists to topple in rapid domino style.

"I've just had a thought," she said to her startled husband. "We don't actually know that Topazz and Soapy *aren't* in that barn. What if

they are? I'm not having my daughter exploded by bombs. Come on!"

With that she climbed the low wooden fence next to the main road where they were parked and began to run across the field back towards the farm. Her husband vaulted it and the two of them were followed immediately by Soapy's mum and dad who had overheard the brief exchange of words.

"Heyo! Be waiting for us!" shouted Olof. He grabbed Pinja and leapt over the fence too.

Only two policemen had been stationed to guard the press and parents gathered along the road and one of them called out, waving his arms.

"Oi, you nutters, you can't do that! Come back! There's missiles and tanks there."

The other officer reached for his radio but was trampled by a giant scrum of reporters and TV crews who rushed to see what was happening. Some of them started filming the escape and then the local newspaper reporter, desperate to get the scoop of his life, jumped the fence and went charging after the six parents, his notepad flapping. The other reporters caught on and began to climb the fence en masse, causing it to collapse with a splintering crack.

Six minutes later, Arvo and Loogi were just starting to think that they were safe. They had crept at least a hundred metres from the soldiers without being seen but now they both looked up, hearing a curious thudding sound in the distance. There, about quarter of a mile away was a group of people running towards them, charging like a herd of wildebeest.

"That is looking like crazy mob," whispered Arvo.

"That is looking like our parents," said Loogi.

Without thinking Arvo turned round and darted over to a large sycamore tree growing up through the hedge next to the lane. He reached for the lowest branch and began to climb.

"Quick, sluggish boy – they are looking more dangerous than army guys!"

Loogi followed and pulled himself up into the tree out of sight.

Three minutes later the Twince watched as six wheezing adults tottered by without looking up, followed by the trailing mob of reporters.

Arvo was about to speak when he was interrupted by the tannoy's now familiar screech blaring towards the barn.

"THIS IS YOUR FIVE-MINUTE WARNING. YOU HAVE FIVE MINUTES TO GIVE UP OR FACE THE CONSEQUENCES."

26
Prankenstein
vs Yankenstein

Inside the barn, a nervous rat jumped down from a bale of straw, scuttled under a potato-harvesting machine and sniffed the air before stealing towards a large pile of mouldy carrots in the corner of the building. It wasn't aware of the two pairs of shifty eyes that watched it, one purple, one yellow.

Prankenstein crouched behind the stack of straw bales, his warty hand gripping a pair of dangling green overalls. The legs had been knotted and filled with fresh pig manure. He peeped out towards the grimy combine harvester at the other end of the building where he knew his enemy was hiding.

Yankenstein sloped out from behind the giant wheel of the harvester and picked up a heavy gas-powered bird scarer cannon.

Both creatures heard the shrill blast of the tannoy from outside.

"YOU NOW HAVE THREE MINUTES TO GIVE YOURSELVES UP. THREE MINUTES."

Their super-sensitive hearing also detected the mechanical grind of gun-turrets being adjusted and weapons being loaded.

Prankenstein stepped out from behind the bales, whirring the stinky overalls above his head like some medieval weapon. He howled and bared his yellow teeth.

Yankenstein too revealed herself, leaping from the shadows into the open space in the centre of the barn, just twenty metres from her rival. She held the bird scarer above her head and screeched, her purple eyes blazing. Prankenstein sneered and jumped up and down, his hairs bristling, his yellow tongue protruding.

Without warning, Yankenstein sprang forward and hurled the bird scarer at Prankenstein. He ducked and it smashed into a one tonne bag of fertiliser. He howled again and unleashed the slimy overalls towards her, globs of hog-poo flying as it sailed past her head and slammed into a roll of barbed wire. Yankenstein hopped and screeched then picked up a barrel of worm pellets and hurled it down the barn. Prankenstein leapt over it then looked around for something to launch back. His eyes settled on the large grunting pig in the corner but before he could grab it a speeding shadow caught his vision and he turned to see Yankenstein lurching through the air towards him, shrieking.

"Urrrrrrhhhhhrrryyyyaaaaa!"

She landed on his shoulders and grabbed his ears, pulling them hard while Prankenstein twisted and fell backwards squashing her against the floor. Yankenstein emptied her nostrils on the back of his head while Prankenstein grappled and

tried to tie her arms in a knot. The two grunted and wrestled with specks of sweat, snot and green saliva spraying as they rolled across the concrete floor of the barn, snarling and straining.

Prankenstein grabbed his adversary's feet to try and swing her into the air but she was too quick and twisted her body to face him and pin his arms to his side. Yankenstein locked her hairy fingers together behind his back, trapping him while Prankenstein stood on her feet so that she couldn't move. The pair were now face to face, straining and pulling, each bursting to get free.

"Eeeeeuuuuummmm," groaned the pranksters but they were of equal strength and both held tight.

After a few seconds, Prankenstein stopped struggling. His mind was not telling him to win but instead to find cheese and yet he also knew there was none of it in the building.

Yankenstein relaxed her grip and for the first time she looked into the yellow eyes just a few inches away. Her brain told her to find eggs but she was strangely transfixed by the face in front of hers.

Prankenstein looked back at the purple eyes staring into his and felt a surge of recognition. He stepped off Yankenstein's feet. She unlocked her fingers and felt the hairs on her arms flatten and stop bristling.

He was drained, almost weak but still held his gaze. The eyes before him were no longer purple but now blue. The face was softer, different. The two became aware of their strength and energy draining moment by moment.

Yankenstein watched as the creature before her became familiar, no more a monster. She reached down and held his hand. It was smooth and clawless. As she did so he let his head rest on her shoulder.

There was a second of silence then a great blare of noise.

"YOUR TIME IS UP!" boomed the tannoy. It was quickly followed by the rumbling roar of a massive diesel engine and a crashing blast as a rolling Centurion tank smashed down the door of the barn.

27
Shock and ooooh

The tank reversed leaving the doors flattened
and a gaping hole at the entrance to the barn.
The other tanks stood in a crescent, each with
a giant gun aimed at the door. In between them
were missile launchers, rocket-powered grenades
and bazookas. Behind, a line of troops stood back
each pointing an automatic weapon at the doorway.

One hundred and fifty metres behind the army,
along the narrow lane leading to the farm, a ring
of police stood around the press and TV crews
who were desperate to try and record the action.
At the side of this mob, pressed against the hedge
were the six alarmed parents, watching and
waiting breathlessly.

In front of this group, standing under a tree
the upright figure of Major-General Vernon
Parker was watching through binoculars and

giving orders on a radio handset. A cluster of advisers leaned towards him and muttered but he wasn't listening.

"Sergeant, move the men into the barn."

His order was received and the quaking soldiers gripped their guns even more tightly and began to walk slowly towards the barn. The sergeant leading the men was wondering what he'd look like on TV when abruptly he put up an arm and called, "Halt!"

He put his radio to his ear and said, "Major-General, sir, there's movement in the barn. Something's coming this way."

The message was picked up by all of the tank crews and missile squads; each soldier's finger tensed against a trigger, ready to squeeze.

The movement in the gloomy barn began to take shape.

Soapy's dad was so desperate to know what was going on that he persuaded Finn to let him climb onto his shoulders so he could see over the heads of the police and press.

"Come on, tell us what's happening," screeched Dove, pulling at his trouser leg.

Mr Thompson held a hand above his eyes. "They – they're coming out of the barn!"

"Who? The creatures?" yelled his wife.

"They're holding hands!"

"WHO?" screamed everybody.

"Soapy and Topazz."

At this point two things happened. First, Finn fainted with shock. As he collapsed, Soapy's dad fell on top of Dove, clonking her to the ground. The second thing was that one of the younger soldiers was so frightened when the two figures emerged from the barn that he accidentally pulled the trigger of his gun. The bullet zinged into one of the thick steel beams holding up the barn then bounced off at over 2000mph fizzing into the nearby tree and snapping off a small branch, the branch that Arvo was hanging on to.

With nothing left to grip, Arvo wobbled then fell out of the tree, landing right on top of Major-General Vernon Parker. Pinja saw her son fall and, unable to control herself, shoved a police officer aside and ran forward shouting, "My son, my son, whichever one you are!"

She dived through the ranks of military advisers and grabbed Arvo, who was being lifted off the general by two brigadiers.

"Who is this prattling woman and this silly boy?" growled the General.

Before anyone could answer, Loogi joined the group. He had been looking down from the tree and wondering what had happened to his brother when his foot slipped. He crashed down through the leaves and landed on top of his mother.

When Olof saw that both of his twin sons were safe he flung up his arms in joy, quite forgetting that he was still holding a heavy wooden mallet. It slipped from his grasp and flew upwards, stopping for a tiny fraction of a second above the gawping reporters, before returning back to earth and landing plum on the head of Soapy's mother with an ugly thump. She had been the only one who still wasn't sure what was going on.

Soapy and Topazz blinked, trying to adjust their eyes to the sunlit sky. They held hands, standing quietly and smiling while six tank guns, eight missiles, fourteen bazookas and seventy-two assault rifles were aimed at them. One by one the rifles were lowered, the tank guns were turned away and the bombs were withdrawn as the army sent soldiers into the barn and confirmed that it was clear.

"The creatures must have escaped – by secret tunnel probably," reported the dazed general by radio to the Home Secretary who was watching from a nearby hill, more confused than anybody. "The main thing is, er, the hostages are safe and well by the look of things."

"I thought you told me there weren't any hostages," she replied.

"Er, no, well, we've found some, Home Secretary."

The emergency medical team arrived and raced forward to check that Soapy and Topazz were all right. A doctor looked them over and prodded the pair a few times.

"You're not hurt at all? Any pain?"

"Yeah," said Topazz, "You're a pain. And where exactly are we? I don't remember coming to World War Three on a farm."

Another medic shone a torch into her eyes.

"What do you remember?"

"Going to sleep and dreaming about eggs. I tell you what – some of my friends told me that Britain was dull but they know zip..."

The first medic looked at Soapy. "Er, we would get you a stretcher but they're all being used." Soapy nodded, "Yes, I can see that."

He watched as a line of beefy paramedics hurried past carrying his mother (complete with Tom and Jerry-style head lump), father, Uncle Finn, Aunt Dove, Pinja, Arvo and Loogi. The Twince gave him a woozy wave as they went by.

BBC News broadcast the whole thing live.

28
Home

A week later, everyone was back at home. Mrs Thompson, a giant bandage around her head, had banned the Daily Mail reporters from her property along with all of the other journalists and TV crews who were camped on the road, trying to find out more about the strangest news story that anyone could remember since that comedian ate someone's hamster.

A taxi-driver was loading bags into the back of his minivan ready to take Dove, Finn and Topazz to the airport where they would fly back to the USA.

The parents hugged each other more quietly than they would normally have done. Soapy and Topazz sat in the kitchen saying their goodbyes.

"I'm glad we made friends again," she said. "Even if what happened went right off the weird scale."

"Yeah, me too," said Soapy. "And you really

believe that those pranks weren't my doing now?"

"Hey, look, those two prank-monsters have been on every TV channel and every website on earth – they must be real and they must have done the pranks. But I still don't get how they kidnapped us and how nobody saw them with us. And why did they do it anyway?"

Soapy swallowed. "No, it's sure a big mystery."

"And why would they take us to a farm? They must be nuts."

He laughed. "Now you are *so* right there."

Topazz shook her head slowly. "And how the heck did they escape when the whole British Army and police force had that barn surrounded? They never found a tunnel or a secret escape route."

Soapy looked wide-eyed. "No, it's, er, amazing."

She moved in close and looked around then spoke in a whisper. "You know what I really think?"

He gulped again. "No."

"That this is all a big conspiracy. You know, some kind of massive government cover up. Loads of people in California say that the CIA faked the moon landings and that Elvis is alive somewhere and that the military have two bodies of aliens that they keep in a cupboard in the White House."

"But why would the Prime Minister pretend that a couple of mad monsters were carrying out epic pranks and abducting kids?"

"Hey, I've seen your Prime Minister – it wouldn't surprise me at all...."

Soapy laughed – after all, it was no more crazy than the truth.

Topazz stood up. "Well, we're going in a minute – I'd better go to the 'loo' and I promise I will NEVER laugh about that word again."

"And I will never joke about bangs," he said, smiling.

While she was gone, Soapy called the Twince to see how they were doing.

Loogi answered. "We are being OK apart from bruises of the multiple kinds. Arvo was disappointed he did not break the limb when he fell – he wanted to visit the fracture clinic to discuss bonce with doctors. Anyway, are you being rid of the visitors yet?"

"No, they're just about to go."

"And they have not done the uncovering of your secret?"

"No, but Topazz thinks it's all a government plot."

Arvo came on the line. "We are worried of the serious kind for you, Soapy."

"Why, because they'll find out the truth? Hey, not even the army and police together managed that!"

"No, boy of irk. Because you have done too much spending time with girl."

Topazz reappeared and Soapy hurriedly shut off the call. Hearing a shout that the taxi was waiting, she held out a hand.

"Well, cousin, as vacations go, it's certainly been one of the more interesting ones...."

He shook her hand and just about managed not to joke that he preferred the hairy one.

"Do you think you'll come over again?" he said.

"I dunno. I think it's been a bit traumatic for Mom and Dad. But, anyway, it's your turn to come and see us in California next time – we can do loads of things in the States."

"Yeah, I can imagine that," he said, wincing at the thought. "Loads and loads..."